Praise for *Rogue Male*

'Nail-biting, boldly plotted ... A mesmeric climax anticipates post-war existential fiction. By any standards: a masterpiece'
The Independent

'While the book is no longer topical, it has lost none of its appeal as a tale of survival against the heaviest of odds'
Daily Mail

'*Rogue Male* is probably the most famous chase thriller ever, influencing an entire generation from Frederick Forsyth to Lee Child'
Catholic Herald

'This is a completely terrific read, a perfect example of its kind and one we'd recommend to lovers of classic thrillers'
Eastern Daily Press

'We are in classic British adventure thriller territory – think Buchan – with an upper-class Englishman showing his stiff upper lip to best effect ... A page-turner if ever there was one!'
Good Book Guide

Born in Bristol in 1900 and educated at Magdalen College, Oxford, Geoffrey Household worked all over the world, including Eastern Europe, the USA, the Middle East and South America, as, among other things, a banker, a salesman and an encyclopedia writer. He served in British intelligence in the Second World War. His other works include *A Rough Shoot, Watcher in the Shadows, Rogue Male* and an autobiography, *Against the Wind*. He died in 1988.

By Geoffrey Household

The Spanish Cave
The Third Hour
The Salvation of Pisco Gabar
   and Other Stories
Rogue Male
Arabesque
The High Place
A Rough Shoot
A Time to Kill
Tales of Adventurers
Fellow Passenger
The Exploits of Xenophon
Against the Wind
The Brides of Solomon and
   Other Stories
Watcher in the Shadows
Thing to Love
Olura
Sabres on the Sand
The Courtesy of Death

Prisoner of the Indies
Dance of the Dwarfs
Doom's Caravan
The Three Sentinels
The Lives and Times of
   Bernardo Brown
Red Anger
The Cats to Come
Escape into Daylight
Hostage – London
The Last Two Weeks of
   Georges Rivac
The Europe That Was
The Sending
Capricorn and Cancer
Summon the Bright Water
Rogue Justice
Arrows of Desire
The Days of Your Fathers
Face to the Sun

ROGUE JUSTICE

Geoffrey Household

An Orion paperback

First published in Great Britain in 1982
by Michael Joseph
This new paperback edition published in 2016
by Orion Books,
an imprint of The Orion Publishing Group Ltd,
Carmelite House, 50 Victoria Embankment,
London EC4Y 0DZ

An Hachette UK company

1 3 5 7 9 10 8 6 4 2

Copyright © Geoffrey Household 1982 and 2016
Afterword © Mike Ripley 2011

A CIP catalogue record for this book
is available from the British Library.

ISBN 978-1-7802-2210-3

Typeset at The Spartan Press Ltd, Lymington Hants

Printed and bound in Great Britain by Clays Ltd, St Ives plc

MIX
Paper from
responsible sources
FSC® C104740

www.orionbooks.co.uk

ROGUE JUSTICE

Prologue

by Saul Harding

In the late summer of 1938 the author of this personal war diary which I have called *Rogue Justice* entered my office limping, scarred and half blind. He had returned from an attempt to assassinate Hitler and would undoubtedly have succeeded if not for a change of wind which delayed his shot for a few fatal seconds. He was caught, left for dead but managed to crawl away and reach England. So dangerous a man could not be allowed by Hitler and his staff to live. Aware that his trail had been picked up and that he was closely followed, he knew that he must disappear for good.

It was then that he came to me, his friend from childhood and his legal adviser, and instructed me to make over his land and all his assets to a cooperative of his tenants, leaving him with enough cash to ensure his safety. I was able to keep in touch with him while he was hiding in deep Dorset, but then I heard no more until a manuscript arrived from France setting out the whole story of his escape, which he asked me to have published as a work of fiction. I had little difficulty in arranging this. The book, entitled *Rogue Male*, was of course valueless as evidence, but if the Foreign Office or the police were ever involved – as well they might be since he had killed two German agents – investigation would quickly show that his account was true. The letter accompanying the manuscript told me that he was about to return to Germany for a second attempt.

I never heard from him again and assumed that he was dead, for I found it hard to believe that, wherever he was, he would not have come racing home to play his part as soon as we were at war. Now at last his recollections explain how he was able to live in Berlin unsuspected. The man chosen to put an end to him was a certain von Lauen, a noted sportsman and shot who had been educated in England and could easily pass in country districts under the name of Major Quive-Smith. When the followed had killed this follower, he took from the body a Nicaraguan passport, genuine, issued in Paris and without doubt a secret precaution in case von Lauen ever fell out with Hitler and found it necessary to escape abroad in a hurry.

My friend, reckless and indomitable as ever, perceived that with some slight alteration in his appearance he could return to Germany on this passport. So he did, and began to stalk his prey with the tenacity of a practised hunter, getting himself known as a prize exhibit of Latin-American admiration for the Nazi system. When war was declared, he was near to a private and deadly interview with Hitler.

Instead of returning home, he persuaded himself that at the cost of his own life he alone could win a more decisive victory than all the allies in arms. I cannot say that he was wrong, but nothing could explain this eager support of the enemy except the truth; and without intimate knowledge of his character and his rare ability to respond to any class and any nation the truth was unbelievable. No other man could have sustained for three years such courage, patience and cunning. It must also be remembered that his passion for vengeance was personal as well as public. Among the monstrous cruelties of the regime had been the inhuman torture of his only love.

Eventually his true identity was discovered, but while temporarily held in Rostock his prison was wrecked by the devastating British air raid of April 1942. It is at this point that he begins his record, written more to justify himself to himself, I think, than with any thought that other eyes might ever read it.

1

My first thought was that in a world where there was any mercy I should have been killed cleanly then and there, for I had no doubt that a more protracted death after days and nights of agony awaited me. Yet I seemed to be the only living thing among the rubble apart from two rats. One of them was squealing; the other was eating its own bowels with apparent appetite. I saw no point in remaining alive with freedom of choice limited to those two alternatives.

When shock had worn off and the only noises were the trickle of falling rubble and the occasional crash of heavier bits of masonry, I stood up cautiously. This provincial gaol where I was temporarily held, stone-built long ago by some prince of Mecklenburg, had taken a direct hit – as I learned much later – from a block-buster or a whole string of bombs dropped by the RAF in the first raid on Rostock. Meanwhile the ancient wooden houses of the town were a giant bonfire uninterrupted, inextinguishable.

The bars of my somewhat antique, underground cell – a dungeon one might call it – still stood up and had sheltered me. On both sides the wall had collapsed. I staggered out and, looking for protection rather than a route to nowhere, felt my way under a massive beam, one end of which was still doing its duty in supporting a part of the floor above me. There I remained in a fantasy of hell. In black night there were tongues of red though I could see no flames, and here and there tongues of silver where crevices in chaos allowed the shafts of a low, bright moon to enter.

First light came early so far north and my tomb of black and red changed to a dim grey in which objects could just be distinguished for what they were. One end of the corridor past the line of cells was open. Slinking along it like a beast through a line of beaters, I entered what had been the office and the guardroom. Hauptmann Haase was sitting at his desk in a chair tilted backwards and held in position by his knees. His head was flattened but the rest of him outwardly intact. The feldwebel, his under-officer, was still recognizable. Another man who must have taken the full force of the blast was – well, the detachable parts of him were scattered about somewhere. I remember him only as a splash on the wall.

That was because my whole concentration was directed towards the hauptmann's head. He must have been chatting with the feldwebel, likely enough about his important prisoner, when a bomb fragment hit him in the face, flattening it beyond recognition and knocking him backwards. His head on its broken neck was hanging over the back of the chair, dripping into the dust and not on to his uniform. The odd spots on his collar could have been red wine not blood. He was the sort of untidy enthusiast who might well have waved his glass about while toasting Hitler and victory.

Even before my partly conscious self had formed any plan, I began looking for that deadly Nicaraguan passport, once the very private property of the so-called Major Quive-Smith, which had enabled me to return from Tangier to France and France to Germany. It was in the top drawer of Haase's desk and easy enough to find. A copy of his signal to Berlin HQ reporting my arrest was also there. At that point conscious human cunning began to take over from animal instinct.

I dragged the body out to my cell and with great care removed the uniform and underclothes. I then dressed him in my own suit. That was very difficult, like putting a full sack into an empty one while at the same time avoiding any stains. For me his uniform was a tolerable fit though baggy at the waist. However, I was unlikely to appear on parade and it would serve.

My last act was to lay the chunk of steel which had killed him close to the body and beneath a ragged hole in the ceiling through which it could have burst its way. With reasonable luck no one could doubt that the corpse in the ruined cell was mine. I would have liked to leave the passport in an inner pocket as conclusive proof of identity but it seemed probable that the Gestapo would have taken it off the prisoner in case he destroyed it. Anyhow there was proof enough. Hauptmann Haase's file gave, with true German thoroughness, details of my arrest and listed the clothes I was wearing, the contents of my pockets including my money, and even the number of the cell in which he had confined me pending the arrival of higher authority. I left the lot in his desk drawer except the money, trusting it would be assumed that someone under cover of the chaos had pinched it. I had hopes of getting away with the exchange of identity if ever I could reach the surface unseen; in such a morgue detailed detective work would hardly be possible, considering the mess of dust and rubble with further collapses as rescuers dug down to the guardroom and the cells. On second thoughts I retained Don Ernesto's passport – deadly if I were searched, but if searched I was doomed anyway.

The climb up to the ground floor was no harder than finding a path up a dangerous slope of scree and boulders, but I could not tell whether I had reached the right level till splintered lengths of floorboard suggested that I had. I saw no other survivor. I did hear cries for help. It was safe to assume that everyone in the upper storeys of this antique police station was either incapacitated or dead. Could I find a way out to the open? Above all, could I find it before the authorities summoned by Haase arrived from Berlin to fetch me?

Somewhere above me I could hear heavy movements and shouted orders, no doubt from a party trying to clear wreckage. Walls released from strain were crumbling around. I took refuge in a fireplace where the bricks of the chimney had jammed and formed a roof which looked as if it might hold until someone poked at it. On this floor scraps of humanity were visible and many more must be under the tons of masonry. When there was a search for Haase's missing body, it would occasion no great surprise if they had to give it up until the whole site was cleared. From the blood beneath and on the back of his chair it would be obvious that he had been badly wounded. A fair guess – at least it would be mine if I were looking for him – was that he had crawled into some hole to die and been buried. As for Don Ernesto Menendez Peraza, so urgently wanted by the High Command, his body could be supplied and its identity authenticated.

There was no way through or over the piles of rubble. I knew little of the effects of bombing; so far as I could see, the blast had opened the building outwards like the petals of a flower and the upper storeys had then collapsed into the central void. I could hear a machine already at work and managed to get close enough to glimpse the jaws of an excavator eating up bricks. It had to be standing outside on hard ground and presumably had a crowd of anxious civilians and military around it so that the sudden appearance of a dusty officer was sure to be observed. In the other direction, towards the centre and away from the excavator, was no conceivable passage; so I returned to the basement to try to plan the unplannable.

I had been escorted down to the basement from the main entrance by a staircase which had now disappeared. There ought to be another way. It was unlikely that food, slops and blankets would all be taken through the imposing entrance hall. An inner court, kitchen and dustbins should exist on or near the level of the corridor which ran past the cells. This corridor, at the opposite end to the guardroom and office, appeared hopelessly blocked. The next cell to mine had suffered similar damage. The iron grille still stood up, but the ceiling had fallen and there was a crumpled corpse beneath it.

Poor devil, I had listened to him throughout the long night. Though our cells were princely and primitive, upstairs there must have been all the Gestapo refinements. My sleepless neighbour had been whimpering like a sick child, murmuring, '*Lotte Liebchen, Lotte Liebchen.*' If he had lived, I doubt if ever again he would have been able to make love to his Lotte. I knew that whimpering. After they caught me rifle in hand at Berchtesgarten I had managed to preserve a Spartan silence while they prised out my nails, but I remember too well the animal grunts and cries, retched not from my brain but from my body as they attended to it, which were the result of panting, broken breath and uncontrollable larynx.

Hours later, when they had, as they thought, killed me, and I had wriggled into the shelter of trees, I heard myself – and can still hear myself – whimpering like my late neighbour.

I squeezed round the iron grille of his cell and could then get at the slope of debris fallen from the floor above into the corridor. This was a fairly solid mass, easy to climb, and I worked my way along the top of it without risk of anything else falling on to me. Then came a mess which at first looked impassable. It had been a kitchen and scullery. I had guessed right.

Profiting by all the experience of the last hours, I looked for some solid object across which a beam or door had fallen leaving a triangular gap through which I could crawl or start to crawl. A concrete pillar that had crashed across the kitchen range provided the gap but beyond was only a buckled, bulging brick wall. Since the pillar provided protection, I dared to batter at the wall with a stout table leg. This was effective. There was a roar of falling masonry, and when the dust cleared I found that I had opened a way into the garage. A partly crushed bus was holding up a bit of the roof. Of two cars, one was shattered and the other appeared to have been blown across the garage. There was a lake of petrol on the floor. I could only thank the lord that my demolition of the party wall had not caused a spark. I had no temptation to explore that garage for a way out into the open.

All this time I had been obsessed by the blind determination to reach the back entrance of the basement. Now, as I became more and more capable of constructive thought, I decided to try the level of the ground floor if I could scramble up to it. A tall slab of wall was standing upright unattached to anything else and seeming as flat as a stage backdrop. The bricks protruding at the side formed a ladder to frighten an ape, but a frightened ape I was anyway. I climbed until I saw that I was about to be outlined against the flames soaring from the town and could go no farther. However, I had caught a glimpse of the courtyard below and the pattern of the hillocks of rubble below me. If I came down a bit and jumped to my left, I should land on an impenetrable mass of devastation which would give me a view of the whole courtyard through the slots and clefts without a chance of being spotted.

The courtyard was full and gave me the impression of onlookers waiting for the worst, apart from a party of police and auxiliaries who were digging frantically with pick and shovel to effect an entrance into the basement. Two ambulances were parked near the outer gate. A fire engine was standing close to the ruins ready for action. I remember that half of me hoped there would be no fire so that the body of Don Ernesto, so carefully prepared for inspection, could be discovered, while another half hoped that the building would catch and make a clean sweep of Hauptmann Haase and his prisoner. With so many people standing about there was no hope of getting from ruins to courtyard and courtyard to gate unobserved. Yes, I could probably stand up to questioning and account for my presence, but afterwards at any inquiry the identity of the unknown Gestapo captain who had inexplicably appeared and disappeared was bound to call for investigation.

I had to divert the attention of the enemy. Garage and fire engine together suggested a way, providing a vivid image of the near future, so long as it allowed any future for me. I did not much care if it didn't, for I had lived with risk so long that I was weary of it. I was at war, had been at war ever since I tried to kill Hitler and very nearly succeeded. Now my country too was at war, and the fact that I was in the heart of the enemy homeland pretending to be a sympathetic neutral no more inhibited me from killing than it would a *franc-tireur* of any resistance movement. So my conscience was clear. The extreme brutality of my act was justified.

What I needed was a box of matches. Hauptmann Haase must have been a non-smoker for there were neither matches nor a lighter in his uniform pockets. I couldn't simply appear from nowhere, walk up to a fireman or ambulance and ask for a light. The person who supplied me had to be silenced. And for the choice of that person convention counted. I would not kill any of the gallant civilian workers who were risking their lives. I wanted an armed enemy.

There was one, and not far away: a real captain in the Gestapo, a gross man compounded of beer, cruelty and cowardice. I could tell all that from his appearance and the fact that he stood by directing workers while calmly smoking a cigarette instead of lending a hand. So he had matches.

I slid down the outside of my pile of rubble into a sort of tangled bay where I could only be seen by someone at the back of the courtyard and behind the ambulances. I had noticed that my chosen victim, strolling importantly up and down in his jackboots and spotless, black uniform sometimes came as far as that. I lay face downwards and pushed my right arm under a slab of wall as if it were hopelessly caught. There I waited for perhaps ten minutes until again he came near enough. Then I cried feebly for help. Of all the risks I had accepted that was the most outrageous gamble. I reckoned that after taking a look at the trapped casualty and appreciating that there was no danger whatever he would do a single-handed rescue in the hope of a decoration when he staggered out of the ruins carrying his comrade. Often in this predatory life of mine I have been able to sum up a potential enemy with even less evidence. Danger gives second sight to the hunted rogue male.

I was half right and half wrong. He took a look at me, was falsely hearty in his words of comfort and said he would bring help. I had rather overdone the stage business. He could well assume that it was impossible for one man to lift the slab and free me. As he turned to go I caught hold of his boot and brought him down. I then killed him. I regret that his death was slower and less merciful than I would have wished, for he was wearing a steel helmet and my only weapon was a brick. I dared not fire Haase's pistol.

Having dragged his body into safe cover and taken off it a useful sum of money I returned to the basement. Scraps of paper were everywhere: wallpaper, files and, best of all, a roll of toilet paper still attached to a pyramid of white tiles. I dropped this through the hole I had opened into the garage, where it unwound itself across the floor, and walked away with the loose end. It made a good fuse, but too fast a fuse; so I built a little fire of wood splinters the flames of which were bound to reach the paper in two or three minutes. Closing my eyes, I lit a match. Nothing happened. There was hardly any smell of petrol where I was, and the slight movement of air ran from kitchen wreck to garage. But I could not he sure.

When the fire was well alight I cleared out over the rubble and back to my bay, where I was protected from heat and explosion – provided the effect of the latter was confined to the garage. I had just tucked myself in under a sheet of corrugated iron when explosion there was and the whole of that flat, still-perpendicular slab of wall came down into the courtyard. Before the dust had cleared, I was running for the gate. The firemen were fully occupied. The ambulance men had taken cover. The courtyard was like a disturbed ants' nest with everyone in movement. I doubt if I was noticed at all. If I was, I should naturally have been mistaken for the crouching, running figure of the late captain.

Outside the gate I turned left, knowing that the other direction would lead me to a crowd in front of the building. I walked fast and importantly down the street, which was empty, probably having been closed by the police. Looking on to the prison courtyard was a wounded, windowless house with no guard on it, so I entered as if on business. What I needed was a clothes brush, a boot brush and a drink. I found all three, shaved off Don Ernesto's moustache and sat down to examine Haase's papers.

I was unfamiliar with the organization of the Sicherheits-dienst, Hitler's security service, for it was not publicized. Haase was commissioned in the Gestapo but wore as well the insignia of the SD, so he was no ordinary political police-man. He appeared to be under the direct orders of the Reich

Security Head Office with authority to do anything and go anywhere subject to reporting to the commanding officer of the district SD.

I hesitated between kitting myself out as a civilian from clothes in a wardrobe or continuing as Hauptmann Haase. The risk of the first alternative was too great. The hounds were hot on the scent of Don Ernesto and the chances were that I should again be arrested by the very first person who ordered me to identify myself. The risk of going ahead as Haase was still worse. For one thing, the photograph on his pass was nothing like me and, though I spoke German perfectly, I did not know the common terms, abbreviations and administrative language of the army. The ideal solution would have been to transfer the photograph from my Nicaraguan passport to the captain's security pass, but the latter had a formidable embossed stamp right across the upper part of it. Only an expert forger could have imitated it.

All the same I decided on Haase and bluff. The essential was to get out of town as soon as possible and an SD officer ought to be able to manage that without showing his pass. Now fairly clean, I left the deserted house and set out for the railway station. My general manner as an officer and no gentleman was authentic enough. I had watched so many of them.

The station was clouded by smoke and in turmoil, for lines had been damaged in the raid and it took a deal of shunting and shouting to get a train together. Meanwhile two battalions of infantry which should have been entrained hours before were patiently making themselves as comfortable as possible in the yards and the forecourt. I got into conversation with several officers and found that as a member of the Gestapo I was not welcome. They gave me a minimum of information, no doubt fearing that it might be my duty to report anyone who gave away details of troop movements. I could only gather that they were separated from their vehicles which had gone ahead before the raid.

I reckoned – rightly as it turned out – that since I did not belong to the units being entrained I should have to obtain some kind of pass, so I hung about the station watching. It looked as if unattached personnel had to apply to the railway transport officer – easy enough so long as I kept a thumb over the photograph and flashed the permit which practically allowed me to travel unquestioned on duty to anywhere. But suppose the transport officer was permanently stationed in Rostock, in which case he would be sure to know Hauptmann Haase? I thought of saying that Haase had urgent duties, had been lightly wounded in the raid and had asked me to find out the first train to the east and get a pass for him. Not good enough. By evening it would be known that Haase's body was somewhere under the rubble, and a signal would be passed down the line to arrest the unknown man who was impersonating him.

Then, thinking of the wrecked garage, I hit on a better story. I had arrived from Denmark that morning on my way to report to Berlin and parked my vehicle at headquarters. It had been completely destroyed in the damnable raid and I wished to go on by train. I had a chat with the transport officer about the iniquity of bombing innocent open cities, which good Germans would never do except in justified reprisal, and got my voucher. Yes, a train should leave in twenty minutes. It would not go through Berlin but I could change at Stettin. And where was it going after Stettin, I asked. Suddenly remembering that I was a security officer, he very properly replied that he didn't know. He never asked for my documents but only for my name. He seemed so twittery that I dared to give him a false one. What an atmosphere of apprehensiveness there was among the stay-at-homes!

Once in the train I had little difficulty in finding out, without asking questions, where it was bound after Stettin. At Posen the units would he reunited with their troop-carriers and trucks, and then they believed to Vienna. They were all in hope that their final destination would be Italy, not the eastern front in the mud of spring. I have never felt anything but respect for the German army. To them what they defended was their country, not its regime born straight from hell.

My railway pass stated my destination as Berlin, but I had no intention of visiting such a concentration of security where my face might conceivably be recognized. I told my fellow travellers that I was on special duty and expected to find further orders for me at Stettin. The sooner I got off the train, the better.

When I left the scene of the disaster, the fire in the garage had been under control and it seemed certain that it would not extend beyond the mountain of rubble which had been the kitchen and reach the guardroom and the cells. Thus Don Ernesto's death would be taken as certain, and his name crossed off the blacklist. But what about Haase? That evening or next day, when the site had been cleared, his superiors would think it odd that there was no trace at all of his body. Blown to bits or a deserter? Inquiries would be made, especially at the station. The RTO would state that he had indeed issued a pass to a Gestapo captain, but his name wasn't Haase. So after futile inquiries up and down the line the fate of Haase was likely to gather dust for some time in a 'pending' file. I could never show his documents to SD or Gestapo but I could to civilians and, if unavoidable, to the military.

*

I have started my story with the bomb that freed me because it is from that point that I date my active participation in the war. But in the interval before my arrival at Stettin I must explain my possession of the Nicaraguan passport and how I used it in the hope of completing my vengeance for the torture and execution of my only love.

After my single-handed attempt to free the world of Hitler and his agitated decision to return the compliment by eliminating me, I re-entered Germany from France in March 1939 travelling from Tangier as Ernesto Menendez Peraza, landowner of Nicaragua. This passport was the very private property of that ingenious and able fellow who passed himself off as Major Quive-Smith. I know now that his true name was von Lauen, that he belonged to a Prussian noble family long settled in Lithuania and that he was educated at Eton. His enthusiasm for Hitler was due to two causes: a belief, natural to a descendant of Teutonic knights, that it was the mission of Germans to civilize eastern Europe – plus any other handy points of the compass – and a bitter anti-semitism inspired perhaps by the number of impoverished Jews in Lithuania.

Von Lauen was given the job of tracking me down. The right man. He was a crack shot who had hunted the forests of Europe and he was out for, let us say, the solitary beast which becomes a man-killer. However, his trust in his employers was not so absolute that he failed to supply himself with the means of escape if necessary. After all, Hitler's early supporters, the Sturm Abteilung, had been mercilessly liquidated in spite of their loyalty. And so, through bribery or friendship, he had acquired this Nicaraguan passport which I took over from his body. The photograph, allowing for a cheap photographer, could conceivably be of me and would serve. But what I did not know and ought to have guessed was that he had told his secret to his wife so that she could join him in Nicaragua if ever he found it advisable to disappear.

Names – what are names in the swift flighting of the sparrow from darkness to darkness? I have been Hauptmann Haase, Menendez Peraza, Bill Smith, yet under these phantom identities always that something which I call myself.

That self now seems to me as futile as his life on earth must seem to a disembodied soul. I lived for sport, for adventure, for killing big game which, thanks to me and my like, may now be risking extinction. My father was British, my mother Austrian. In those gentle and self-satisfied days before the first war, intermarriage between ancient lines was as common as in the royal family. I was thus perfectly bilingual with a fair smattering of other languages.

When I arrived in Berlin as Ernesto Menendez Peraza I settled down in a small furnished flat in the suburbs. My identity was never questioned, nor was my story that as a mature student of politics I wished to study the ideals and organization of National Socialism. I visited libraries, attended lectures, asked explanations from minor officials and cultivated the society of the scum who believed in their divine Führer and the mission of the Reich. In France I had taken a quick course of Spanish, which I now perfected by lessons from a Mexican secretly and in another part of the city until I could speak fluently the language of my passport. Meanwhile I was careful to avoid Spaniards and Latin Americans. I had good reason to hope that when I had established my bona fides I might obtain an interview or at least be given a privileged seat at some function where Hitler was due to scream his rages.

I had once thought that a rifle on a roof was the most efficient method of silencing that scream. It was the plan of an experienced hunter without enough knowledge of police protection. I assumed that in their precautions against bomb and handgun they might have overlooked the rifle and telescopic sight in the hands of a crack shot; but they had not. And the weapon itself was impractical. Yes, Don Ernesto could buy one and take it home. But what then? There was no hope of strolling with it to the chosen roof top or of secreting it there beforehand. Security was far too efficient.

Life did not appear to me as futile as it was, for the ultimate object was always in the forefront of my mind. The months of play-acting, each one showing a slight advance, absorbed me. I began to cultivate higher circles than the scum of the party with which I had started. Living very simply, I had enough money. While hiding in England I had used little of the five thousand pounds which I had obtained from my solicitor and I had naturally relieved von Lauen of the considerable sum of secret funds which he carried on him and was not in a position to spend at the bottom of the Severn.

As an enthusiast for the world-wide influence of the Reich, I began to talk of establishing dictatorships on the Pacific coast of Latin America which would rule and expand under the guidance of the Nazi Party. This nonsense was taken seriously and I was asked to lecture on the right of the superior man to extend his rule over Indians, negroes and mestizos. The landowners of pure Spanish blood would, I said, welcome the fellow Aryan and his tradition of good government. It was no more absurd than other Nazi dreams, and I delighted in my inventions and parodies. Now known as a propagandist, I was getting nearer and nearer to Hitler – near enough, I hoped, to be able to use my bare hands to break his neck before I was shot down.

And then came war. At long last my country had become my ally, and there was I stranded in enemy territory and unable to take part. As a neutral I could reach Switzerland,

Sweden or Spain. But what then? What were the chances of being shipped or flown to England? I had no fear of returning home. There was no conceivable reason why I should be accused of my two kills. The police had been hot on my trail and my appearance had been exactly described – a man with a damaged eye, always wearing gloves – but the identity of the criminal was unknown. The eye was now fairly normal and my nails had grown back.

Meanwhile the peoples of peace at any price suffered defeat after defeat. But I could not see my country ever accepting defeat. If only I were home, with what cruelty and cunning I could lead a unit of resistance or attack! And for Nazi Germany victory was not enough. Hidden from the people behind impenetrable, triumphant lines of swastika banners, the slaughter of the helpless began. The plain, decent citizen could not have guessed its extent but, among the excrement of the Reich with which I drank and babbled, rumours of the concentration camps and the liquidation of communists and Jews circulated and were highly approved. I could bear no more of it. The fanatical patience of three years was exhausted; vengeance on the man was beyond my powers. Vengeance on a poisoned nation was not.

I decided that it was by Denmark and Sweden that I would try to get home. I hadn't a hope of doing it legally. To obtain the exit permit I should first have to apply to the consul-general in charge of Central American interests for clearance. So far, I had had the least possible contact with him and, as he spent half of his days in sleep and the other half at parties, he had never bothered to keep track of me. But he happened to be a Nicaraguan who probably knew the names of all the members of landowning families in his small country. I foresaw questions I could not answer. He would provide me with a comfortable chair and a drink while from another room he telephoned the police.

Through influential friends I had no trouble in getting as far as Denmark as a known Nazi sympathizer and propagandist. Once in Copenhagen I was disappointed to find that there was no passenger service at all between Denmark and Sweden. There was, however, more trade than I expected. The heavy and essential imports of iron ore and timber went directly from Sweden to north German ports, but coasters came over on the short passage from Malmö with light cargo and returned with anything that Germany could spare and Sweden needed. It might be possible to cross as a stowaway, provided I was free to enter Sweden on arrival.

So I applied to the Swedish consul for a visa to enter his country, which he gave me, at the same time warning me that I should never be allowed to leave without a formal German permit. That I knew only too well, but I was determined to be carried across the straits without any permission but my own. I welcomed with all my heart the straight challenge to straight action after three hateful years of intrigue and hypocrisy.

Since the enemy kept up a diplomatic fiction that Denmark, though occupied, was still an independent country, the port police were officially Danish and allowed small parties of seamen to come ashore. I followed several such groups and sat near them in cafés, but no faces or voices tempted me to gamble. I had to be very careful whom I approached, avoiding any Swede or Dane who was expressing too loudly his pro-British sentiments. It was certain that the Gestapo would have their spies and *agents provocateurs* in the bars.

On the third day I noticed that out of a party of six Swedes two were foreigners, to judge by their manner and way of speaking. After a while the two went off by themselves. I tailed them at a discreet distance, passed and re-passed and found that they were talking in Spanish. Worth a try! When they entered another bar I stood alongside and introduced myself as a South American. As soon as the comradeship of the language had been established, I invited them to have a bite to eat with me. Over the table I got their story of how the devil two Spaniards could be working on a Swedish ship.

It turned out that they had been in the defeated republican army and were among the few refugees who were evacuated to Russia. Like most foreign communists, they loathed their paradise and, as Spaniards, were horrified by the cold of the Arctic circle, for they had been assigned jobs – possibly in the hope that they would die – in one of the little ports of the White Sea. From there they escaped to Finland and applied to go on to Sweden, where a token handful of Spanish refugees had been accepted.

I could fearlessly tell such men as these that I, too, wanted to escape but had not a hope of getting a permit.

'Easy!' they insisted. 'Let's start by pretending to be drunk and raising hell. We'll all three be arrested and taken back on board. You will look for your pass and swear some son of a whore has pinched it out of your pocket. We'll keep on telling the police that you're a member of the crew, and if they take you back with us the captain will confirm it.'

I objected that he would do nothing of the sort, and they asked if I spoke English. When I said that I did, they wanted to know if it was good, proper English that an Englishman speaks. I assured them it was. Then they nodded and winked at each other and, before I could protest, started the hell-raising, singing the Internationale, breaking two glasses and chucking smorgasbord at the ceiling. Thereafter everything went as they had foretold except for a deadly moment when the Danish police refused to take me back on board with them. But they linked arms with me, one on each side, refused to let go and the police decided that their fellow Scandinavians on the ship might as well sort it out and save them trouble.

I could do nothing. I was appalled at the speed with which the worst had happened. We were escorted through the controls, marched on deck and handed over to the first officer. I expected him to say at once that he had never set eyes on me in his life, but before he could explode my two friends started to sing out with good Spanish fury, 'We demand to see the captain, sir. We demand to see the captain. We have been wrongly arrested, sir. We demand to see the captain.'

I have no Swedish but the meaning of the words was simple enough to guess.

Members of the crew on duty were hanging about and grinning. I had the impression that the two Spaniards were appreciated as entertaining ship's pets and were well aware of it. The general mood was all in their favour, for it was possible that they had been run in not for being drunk but as old enemies of General Franco who had expressed themselves too forcibly. The mate, who had no wish to get involved in an international incident, took all three of us before the captain without bothering to denounce me.

We were stormed at for getting drunk on foreign soil, and to my astonishment he made no difference between us. I let my friends do the talking, keeping quiet except for occasional protests and exclamations in Spanish. I was told to shut up. The police, content with the captain's apparent recognition of me, departed. The two licensed jesters were ordered back to duty. I was shown into a bare cabin which was promptly locked.

I was left to myself, cursing my folly in trusting – though I could hardly help it – to a pair of lunatics, wishing that I had tried Switzerland, wondering how much pain I should suffer after my true identity had been discovered until it was decided that I could be given a final kick and left to die. The captain, in the presence of police, had evidently been extremely discreet in case the ship were accused of assisting and harbouring enemies of the state. But I was sure that before he sailed with his cargo of fertilizers he was bound to hand me over in his own time to the right person.

He came into the cabin, locking the door behind him.

'And now who are you?' he asked in German.

'A Nicaraguan and a neutral like yourself,' I answered, showing my passport duly visaed for Sweden.

'Then you could have obtained permission to leave. Why did you persuade these men to smuggle you on board?'

'We were so happy in speaking our own language, sir.'

'I did not ask you how you persuaded them, but why.'

'I was unlikely to get permission to leave.'

'Your passport is false?' He suddenly snapped at me in perfect English.

'I'm afraid it is, sir.'

'How is it you speak Spanish?'

'Because I was born in the Argentine.'

'What is your true name?'

At last I could see what had been in his mind as a possibility and that he was ready to help. He may have been an agent of some underground organization or simply pro-British. I was not prepared to give my true name until I was safely in our embassy; so I gave him a false one, saying that I had been taken prisoner at Calais in 1940.

'Very well. Congratulations! I shall keep you locked up until we dock and I shall then send for an officer of your consulate and hand you over to him. And I ask you to give me your word of honour that you will never tell anyone except your own authorities that I accepted you on board.'

He handled the tricky situation very cleverly. While I was still locked up, the vice-consul must have come on board and the necessary arrangements made. In case German agents were carrying out a routine watch on the dock gates, as they certainly would be, I went on shore with other members of the crew including the two Spanish refugees. After a further interval to throw off any followers, I was put straight on to the train to Stockholm and taken by car to a quiet residence outside the city.

I remember what joy it was to be free. I could not sleep for joy. There had been some reserve among the British deputies who dealt with me but it was to be expected. Next day I should be able to explain myself to someone in authority.

Next day came and still another before I was interrogated. I think the person who visited me must have been the British military attaché. I told him at once that my claim to be an escaped prisoner-of-war was a lie. He had known my father and was very friendly, though warning me that nobody was taken on trust by what he called the intelligence wallahs. I then had to explain how I came by the passport of Ernesto Menendez Peraza which enabled me to avoid internment.

I had of course thought up a possible story. My mother, as he knew, came from an ancient family of diplomatists and soldiers. At the time of the declaration of war I had been, I said, in the remote eastern province of Czechoslovakia, where the family still held a remnant of their former estates near Uzhgorod. None of us believed that Britain and Germany were on the verge of war. If the British government had not fought when Czechoslovakia was invaded, why on earth should it fight for Poland? I was caught, still hesitating, in enemy territory, a long way from organized evacuation of British citizens, and was certain to be interned for the duration of the war.

So I claimed to have been hidden on the estate. A Nicaraguan passport was bought for me and I had been able to live as a harmless neutral.

My interrogator was surprised that I had never been recognized by old friends. I answered that as a schoolboy I had spent holidays with my maternal grandparents (which was true) but had had no intimate friends, only aquaintances who were unlikely to recognize the grown man.

'Why did you not try to escape earlier?'

'Because I could not find any safe method of doing so which would not have got my family into severe trouble if I were caught.'

'I see. Now you will understand that since you are not a prisoner-of-war there must be more formalities before we can issue a British passport and arrange to send you home. Stay where you are for the present, and don't go out beyond the garden. Ask for anything you want. And in a day or two you will be interviewed by the passport control officer.'

I did as I was told, realizing that reference back to London for details of my birth certificate and all that was known of my past must take time. On the third day a youngish man – but with deep creases on each side of his cordial, smiling mouth – came to visit me, plonked us both down in comfortable chairs, not even wholly facing each other, and began his questions. I remember every terrible word of that interrogation, remember it better than my interrogation at Berchtesgarten. This professional was as good as theirs, and, from my point of view, the suffering was more cruel than physical pain.

'I understand that when asked why you did not try to escape earlier you replied that you were afraid of getting your relatives into trouble.'

'That is so.'

'But if they were able to buy you a false Nicaraguan

passport surely they could have bought from the same man an endorsement which would have enabled you to get an exit permit? Then you could have left Germany legally.'

I answered that their contact had returned to Central America and that the present representative was honest as well as pro-German.

'When did you leave England?'

'In June 1938.'

'Directly to Germany?'

'No. I spent some months in Greece and the Middle East and then went to stay with my relations.'

My interrogator suddenly broke into Spanish, speaking with the clipped and racy accent of, I believe, Madrid. We chatted away cordially for a minute or two and then he asked, 'Did you speak Spanish before or did you learn it when you got your passport?'

'Daily lessons while I was waiting for the passport and afterwards.'

'And very sensibly you chose a South American to teach you, I see.'

'Yes, a Mexican.'

'In Uzhgorod? One would not have thought there was any demand for a teacher of Spanish.'

'There wasn't. I think I was his only pupil.'

'What did he do for the rest of the time?'

I hesitated, scenting danger.

'Lived on his Czech wife, who had some money.'

'And you trusted a type of that sort to keep his mouth shut?'

'He didn't know I was not German.'

'But if you had been there so long before the war with no reason to hide, country neighbours must have known you were English.'

'If they did they said nothing.'

He switched back to English.

'For fourteen months before the war you wrote no letters.'

'I must have done. I don't remember.'

'My inquiries suggest that none of your friends knew what had become of you and assumed that you had disappeared into Africa or Asia and might be dead.'

'Letters do get lost,' I answered weakly.

'From Greece and Czechoslovakia? Quite good postal services, I believe. Now when you were caught by the outbreak of war and staying with your relatives, how close were you to the frontiers of Romania and Hungary?'

'About twenty-five miles from Hungary and sixty from Romania.'

'Wild country?'

'Yes. Hills and forest.'

'I should have thought that a man of your experience would have been able to slip over into neutral territory on foot.'

'They all considered it too dangerous.'

'Less dangerous than letting you risk your life with a false passport in Germany? By the way, your Nicaraguan passport was issued by the Paris consulate in 1938, not 1939.'

'The date was false.'

'Now please let me have the truth. As it is, I can only report that you entered Germany in 1938, returned in 1939, and that you wished to keep it quiet. Was it a political reason that took you there?'

Foolishly I had expected that my word would be sufficient. I had never expected close questioning. The holes in my story were obvious. The only thing left was to confess.

'The purpose of both journeys was to assassinate Hitler.'

'I see. What a pity you didn't! Have you any proof of that?'

I had not. It was unthinkable to let anyone know of my intention to kill a head of state in time of peace. Even when I managed to return to England after they had left me for dead, I could not even allow Saul, my dear friend and solicitor, to know exactly where and by whom I had been torn and tortured. There was always the danger that I could be accused of acting as an agent of the British government. That was precisely what von Lauen, in his avatar of Quive-Smith, had demanded that I confess in writing.

'I have no proof.'

'When did you change your opinion of the Führer?'

'I have never changed it.'

'We have fairly accurate reports of the movements and interests of neutrals within Germany. Not from unreliable spies. From neutral diplomatists and journalists, most of whom are pro-British.'

'I have not been in touch with any of them.'

'Possibly not. I wished to remind you that Germany isn't entirely closed. I have some of Ernesto's newspaper articles and reports of his speeches.'

'All that was to enable me to get close to Hitler.'

'And did it?'

'No. In the end I decided I was wasting my time and ought to be serving my country directly.'

'Certainly you ought. And you really believed that with your record we should allow you into wartime Britain?'

'But I am British!'

'I don't doubt it. What I do not know is whether you are one of those arrogant members of the upper class who are proud to wear black shirts and betray humanity for the sake of power which the people will never give them, or perhaps you are a paid German agent provided with a suspiciously stupid German story – in fact, whether you are a conscious or unconscious traitor. Either way they found you a useful man, speaking German and English perfectly and Spanish well enough to be a convincing neutral. Which are you?'

'Neither. I have told you the truth.'

'You have told me a pack of lies. And England in wartime would be better without you.'

I replied, angry for the first time, that he could not prevent me from returning, and added that if I were a German agent I would not have entered Sweden illegally and reported at once to my own people.

'I think you would. German intelligence has that much sense. But if the best story they could invent for you was this nonsense of a single-handed attempt to assassinate the most heavily guarded gangster in Europe, they underrated us or perhaps wished to get rid of you. Give that some thought when you are returned with thanks!'

'You cannot return me!'

'That is up to the Swedish government. So far as we are concerned, you are Ernesto Menendez Peraza and your passport is in perfect order. I have no doubt that the Swedes will discreetly slip you back into Copenhagen without any need to state how you got there.'

It was not as easy as all that. I was handed over to some operatives of what I presume was the Swedish secret service, who accepted me as a pro-German Nicaraguan and asked me why I had entered Sweden illegally. It was no good claiming to be British when my own people had rejected me, so I said that I had hoped to be allowed into England where I might be able to get home to Nicaragua if I could find a ship that would take me as far as the United States.

The Swedes of course knew how I had arrived but couldn't think what to do with me. They would have liked to send me straight back to Denmark, but if they did they would have to explain how I had smuggled myself into Sweden with willing help. That would be deadly for me and embarrassing for them. They talked to me quite frankly. I could be secretly shoved over the frontier into German-occupied Norway and left to fend for myself, or I could stay in Sweden under close supervision until there was a chance of shipping me across the Atlantic, which might be arranged later in the year. I did not like either alternative and came up with a simple solution.

'I am authorized to reside in Berlin,' I said. 'I have a permit to visit Denmark. I have the correct visa to enter Sweden. All this you can see from my passport. The only thing I do not have is the German exit permit. Why don't you forge it? It will never be noticed and I can then return openly.'

This appeared to the good Swedes rather too disreputable, but they went into a huddle and agreed that it might be done. So I was put on a ship from Gothenburg and landed at Copenhagen with my papers in perfect order.

I returned to my hotel to pick up my bag and pay my bill. A risk which had to be taken, since I should have been reported to the police as either missing or having skipped without paying. My explanation that I had unexpectedly fallen in with old friends from Berlin and written to the hotel that I should be away for a few days was accepted, I thought, too easily. Of course it was. My arrival had been reported as soon as I set foot in the place.

While I was having lunch I was called down to the manager's office, where I was alarmed to find not Danish civil police but two of the Gestapo. They checked the details of my passport and arrested me. No reason was given. No questions were put. I supposed that my unauthorized visit to Sweden must have become known, though I could not believe that either the Swedes or my compatriots had given me away.

I was escorted for six silent hours down to Rostock by road and ferry with a sergeant sitting beside me all the time and refusing to enter into conversation. The car stopped outside that princely gaol. My body was signed for and I was taken to my cell. That I was in danger of everything that Nazi brutality could do to me was obvious. But why?

Some hours later – just to give me time to think over crime and punishment – I was taken before Hauptmann Haase. He came pretty straight to the point.

'Were you born in Bondriza, Nicaragua, as your passport states?'

I answered that I was and that it could be confirmed, knowing that the only chance of communicating with Nicaragua would be by radio, and that it would probably take months to get any confirmation from what was probably a remote village if the consul whom von Lauen had bribed knew his job.

'You entered Germany from France in April 1939. Account for your movements between the time you left Nicaragua and arrived in France!'

'I was travelling in the Americas and then came to Europe. I will try to give you exact dates but it will be difficult. And I must remind you that I am well known as a sympathizer with your country and a devoted admirer of your Führer.'

'Where did you learn to speak faultless German?'

A very awkward question, that! I had to invent a German school in Costa Rica and the name of its headmaster.

'Have you ever been in England?'

'Only when I landed there from New York.'

He said nothing about Sweden or the hotel in Copenhagen. I did not like that at all, but it still did not occur to me what accusation I had to answer.

'To whom does this passport really belong?'

'To me of course.'

'Not to a certain von Lauen?'

This was so unexpected that eyes or face must have given me away though I tried to remain unmoved.

'But I have been in Berlin for three years and my passport has never been questioned.'

'Never, you swine, till you came in from Sweden, but you are caught at last — ' He jumped up and hit me across the face. 'You a friend of the Führer! But you have forgotten the true heart of the German wife and mother. Again and again she asked for news of her husband, von Lauen. The only reply the state could give her was that it knew nothing. And then, three long weeks ago, she told us that in order to serve the fatherland should he find himself abroad in time of war he had bought a Nicaraguan passport and gave us date and number. All were warned to look out for it. Every post in the Reich. This is it! You are a spy and an impostor. I would like to deal with you myself but my orders are to send you to Berlin to account for all the filth you have committed. They will soon have the truth out of you there.'

The heroic German wife had certainly invented a good story. She had never mentioned her husband's private passport because she hoped to join him some day across the Atlantic. But, as never a word from him came and knowing that he had been employed as an agent abroad, at last she gave away his secret and put the best possible interpretation on it.

And so I was taken back to my cell to brood over the inevitable outcome that I should be recognized as the hunter who had attempted to send the holy Führer to the pit of hell reserved for him, whom von Lauen had tracked down from London to Dorset and then to the bestial hole in that deserted lane where at last I had killed him.

I have written how the raid on Rostock saved me and how

it came about that I was prevented from joining the armed services of my country till it was too late. Therefore I was determined after my escape to enter the war alone, to kill alone and myself to receive death alone.

What had begun as a personal vendetta became my response to all those guilty of hurling a civilized world into war, of murdering political opponents, of enslaving defenceless workers, and above all of herding into slaughter-houses a helpless, warm-hearted, gifted people whose religion and customs slightly differed from the national norm. My use of arms was as justifiable as if I had been under military command.

2

When I walked away from the troop train into Stettin goods yard, leaving, so far as I knew, no clue or curiosity behind, I was very far from feeling the happy warrior. I was a badly wanted man in the heart of enemy country with no assets but a uniform and a headquarters pass with the wrong photograph on it. No strategy at all could be planned; tactics depended on the single weapon of Haase's loaded pistol and a spare magazine.

The first of my difficulties was money. All I had was what I had recovered from Haase's desk, plus the small sum taken from the Gestapo captain whom I had killed – enough for a week or so but hardly a war loan. A visit to my Berlin bank was impossible since Haase had confiscated my cheque book and made a note of it. I could eat for a while but dared not attempt to get free quarters in barracks or officers' mess. As for hotels, I would have to find out very cautiously what privileges, if any, an officer of the SD enjoyed. On the credit side it seemed that bluff would secure me free travel. So the next task was to put as much distance as possible between Stettin and myself, disappearing into the confusion of Hitler's Reich.

As I hesitated, lonely, lost and separated from all the military activity on the station, I saw a sergeant and corporal of the Gestapo hurrying down the line towards me and was seized by unreasoning panic. Shoot my way out or run? My hand was already on my holster. I had to remind myself that I was no longer Don Ernesto but the superior officer of these fellows, correctly uniformed and unquestionable. But it was not until they gave me a smart salute in coming abreast that I recovered self-confidence.

I stopped them and asked what their duties were. They took this as a rebuke and one of them said, 'We thought it would be all right, sir, if we went over to the buffet for a bite when they told us that the train would be late.'

I longed to ask what train, but thought I ought to appear all-knowing.

'You are travelling on duty?'

'Escort, sir. Guards on the prisoners are changed here.'

'That's a job for the SS, not us,' I said. 'But I suppose they can't take time off from running in Jewish girls.'

They dutifully laughed.

'Well, sir, it's not a convoy – just four dirty Poles being sent to do some honest work at Auschwitz. They won't enjoy it, they won't!'

'Oh, those four! Yes, I was present when they were caught. That must be the reason why I am ordered to accompany you. Further interrogation probably.'

Safe, untraceable departure from Stettin was being offered to me on a plate and I accepted it. I had never heard of Auschwitz and returned to my arrival platform for a look at the map displayed there. It appeared to be the place the Poles called Oswiecim, which was a junction for several lines. The expected train probably went on to Cracow and so would I.

I drifted back to the wrong side of the troop train, where I could keep watch on the waiting escort and would be inconspicuous in case some officer turned up to inspect. In ten minutes the Cracow train came in and the guard on the prisoners was relieved. As soon as the new pair had entered the reserved compartment, I followed. Wishing them a good journey I went forward to the first class. I was so obviously connected with the movement of criminals that no one was impertinent enough to ask for my pass or ticket.

Of the four prisoners, two might be described as in comparatively good health after being entertained by the Gestapo. One of them was obviously in pain, doubled up with his forearms on his knees; the other had half his face so badly bruised that I suspected a broken cheekbone. The remaining two were spread out on the floor. Evidently the guard had been unwilling to share seats with such *Schweinerei*. They were also conveniently placed for kicks.

It was not only pity that compelled me to set them free. I needed them. If they were Poles and guilty of belonging to some underground organization or even of some quite mild resistance to the occupying power, they might be able to help me. Night was coming down. We had passed Breslau over an hour ago, and the train was gathering speed over a flat and melancholy plain with an occasional gleam of water.

The difficulty was how to dispose of the guards. I was still in those days legally minded – in the sense that my solitary war should obey the rules of public war. The guards were in enemy uniform and could therefore be killed. On the other hand they were not in action and I was in no danger from them. I decided that they should arrange their own decease. A touch of hypocrisy there, I think. The fact was that I dared not fire two shots in case the sound was heard before I had time to clear up.

When it was dark and window blinds drawn, I entered that closed and sinister compartment with a cheerful word. The two escorts jumped up. By this time I knew the Gestapo to the bottom of the sludge where their hearts had been.

'I will now tell you why I am here,' I said. 'These prisoners are to have an accident while trying to escape. We will throw them out, taking care that they fall on their heads.'

Then, drawing my pistol, I told the poor devil with the broken face to stand up, ordered the sergeant to get those fellows off the floor and the corporal to open the door halfway and be careful he didn't fall out.

They were startled and hesitated, but the orders had come smartly in succession and they had only time to obey and not to think. The attitude of the prisoners was also convincing. One of the Poles on the floor cried out in horror. The other three showed no fear but only proud, sullen acceptance.

The corporal opened the door and had some trouble controlling it against the wind with no firm grip. I slammed the butt of the pistol down on his head and kicked him out. Then I whipped round and covered the sergeant. I had not worked this move out. He had only to shout or pull up the blinds on the inner windows or show fight in any way. But hatred gave wings to the prisoner who was doubled up in pain. He undoubled himself, leaped at the sergeant and was intelligent enough to get an arm over his mouth. The rest of the walking wounded were on him in a flash, and he joined his partner on the permanent way head-first, so that I hoped for the best.

'Don't be afraid and shut the door!' I said, covering them from the inner end of the compartment since I was not too sure that they might not be tempted to send a third uniformed criminal after the other two.

I let them know at once that I was British not German. Broken Face replied in English, which he spoke very well, and, when I told him so, he seemed satisfied with me, though for the moment nobody trusted anybody else.

I handed him my headquarters pass.

'Look at that! Treat it with respect for we shall need it. Look at the photograph! Do you think I am Hauptmann Haase?'

He said something in Polish to the other three, who relaxed. Poor Doubled-Up collapsed in agony with the return of the pain which he had momentarily forgotten in action.

'When shall we get off and disappear?' I asked. 'You know the country and I don't. We are now about half an hour from Auschwitz, where you were going, so the Cracow train will stop there. I can probably manage to have an emergency stop earlier. Can any of you say where we should have the best chance of getting clear away? Then, if you can find me a safe hide-out, civilian clothes and a bag to put this damned uniform and boots in, I will look after myself and not be an embarrassment to you and your friends.'

I was accepted. Broken Face, with Polish generosity, embraced and thanked me as a tear like a raindrop on black rock ran down his bruise.

They went into a huddle, talking together in swift, musical Polish – a language of which I had no experience and had always misjudged because of its outlandish spellings. Meanwhile I prepared for trouble. Our operation had been reasonably silent, allowing for the rattle of the wheels on worn track, but the corporal had let out a scream before he hit the ground.

Sure enough, the train guard came along and knocked at the door, which I half opened so that he could not see the whole compartment.

'Everything all right, sir?' he asked. 'It has been reported to me that someone may have fallen from the train.'

'Thank you. Everything is under control. One of these prisoners managed to open the outside door and shouted for help. He has been attended to. You can be sure he will not do it again.'

He shivered slightly, saluted and went away. They knew,

they knew all right, what sort of a police force Himmler had trained.

Doubled-Up told us that Cracow was his home and everyone there knew that a concentration camp was being built at or near Auschwitz, so guards and transport would certainly be at the station to receive us. Broken Face added that he had once been duck shooting over the nearby marshes, that there was little cover and he doubted if we could reach forest before we were surrounded and caught. The two who had been on the floor were crushed and demoralized, suggesting that their case was hopeless and that they should all commit suicide before treatment for murdering guards.

That put some spirit into Broken Face, who snarled that he was damned if he would die by his own hand if there was still a chance of killing a German. He proposed that we should stay on the train till Cracow if at all possible. Then we could perhaps reach a telephone and get in touch with the underground.

I thought that there was little chance of being able to stay on the train, which would be thoroughly searched at Auschwitz when escort and prisoners never got off. Meanwhile the two bodies on the line might be discovered at any moment so that whatever we did must be done quickly. Our aim should certainly be Cracow. If we could be told a safe method of leaving the city, the Carpathian mountains were not far off and I had once known them well.

The committee of life and death agreed that I should not attempt to stop the train, drawing attention to ourselves by getting off in the middle of nowhere, stumbling a little through marshes and streams while the bodies were discovered and the whole military district alerted. We had better trust to luck and my uniform on arrival at Auschwitz. If I had been alone, I would rather have tried the marshes.

So could I go on pretending to be in charge of the prisoners and say that I had put the regular guard under arrest at Breslau for some crime or other and handed them over to an SS detachment? Ingenious, but it wouldn't do. The reception party was bound to have a word with the train guard.

Another alternative we considered was to slide off the train as it slowed down to enter the station and scatter in the dark, perhaps boarding the train again as it pulled out and clinging to whatever handhold there was. Two objections to that. First, at least three of them were not fit enough – even if unhurt – to pick themselves up and run. Second, we could not know how brightly station and yard would be lit.

Broken Face, that gallant fellow, was more concerned for my safety than his own. If I kept up my pretence of being in sole charge of the prisoners, he said, I should be able to hand them over and disappear before my story of arresting the guards at Breslau was exposed as a lie.

I replied that I would rather open a battle, that I was a fine shot and would kill four or five of them before they got me.

'That wouldn't do any of us any good, sir,' he said. 'Now take my advice and have nothing to do with us. You are an officer of the Sicherheitsdienst travelling to Cracow on his own business. Keep out of the way! The chaps who are waiting for us will know in what compartment we are and may take us off straightaway without a word to the train guard.'

Doubled-Up, who had lived in Cracow, thought it was quite likely. Whatever was going on, the camp was dead secret and the public was not allowed to know anything.

'But, if there was no guard on you at all, why didn't you escape?' I asked.

'What was the use? We have no strength. And we knew the guards could not be far off. Their kit is still here.'

So it was decided. I was to be entirely detached from them

and waiting for a chance to intervene if ever the situation allowed. It was the slenderest hope. They very movingly prayed for me and for themselves.

I returned to my first-class compartment and kept watch as we pulled in to Auschwitz. No Gestapo guard was waiting on the platform. I looked at the other side of the train. A sergeant and a private of the SS, both armed with machine pistols, were walking straight for the prisoners, who were ordered out with their hands behind their heads. There were sharp questions and answers. I presumed that one of the Poles was saying that he didn't know where the guards were, probably somewhere up the train, because their kit was still in the compartment. The prisoners were marched away. Duty apparently came first, and the missing comrades would be routed out later.

The yards were largely in shadow. Beyond the limping prisoners there seemed to be a ramp on which a truck was standing. I walked quickly, and with the importance proper to an officer of the SD, round the back of the train and tucked myself in behind buffers, where I could see without being seen. The party of four was pushed – thrown would be a better word – into the closed truck and the rear door fastened with an iron bar. The sergeant then began to return to the station, leaving the other fellow standing by the truck. No one else was there, so he was the driver.

This seemed to be the end. There was not even the slenderest hope. As soon as the sergeant arrived, the train guard and station staff would start telephoning. The bodies would be discovered on the line and the SD officer exposed as a fraud. Inevitable. But out of my sense of utter failure came sudden inspiration. By God, if the bodies had not yet been discovered, let them be discovered now, when it suited me!

I met the sergeant on his way, as if appearing from the back of the train.

'You there! Two bodies of our men have been seen on the line. Immediate investigation! Have you got any men with you?'

'One, sir.'

'Get him at once to help you. Search the compartment and report to me. Never mind your prisoners for the moment. They can't get out.'

He called for his driver, who came running, and both climbed at once into the prisoners' compartment. I made for the truck as fast as I could without actually running. It started sweetly and we were off. The Cracow road was marked. I reckoned we should have a useful lead while the sergeant was bullying the train guard, trying to find out whether the captain had really been in charge of the missing guards and whether he was the same captain who had ordered immediate investigation, and what the hell was going on.

My Poles had been quite right in their description of the locality. On foot and across country escape would have been hardly possible, nor was the Cracow road at all promising, since both ends of it could easily be blocked. Marsh, ponds and muddy streams were everywhere, crossed by causeways or small bridges. In the night our course over this maze of fenland appeared more confusing than it really was, owing to extensive drainage works. Banks of spoil loomed up in the headlights, together with the misty shapes of digging machines and bulldozers which might be on or off the road, and forced me to slow down. At the time I assumed that the enemy was building some sort of anti-tank ditch to hold up a Russian advance. It never occurred to me – and how should it in a more or less Christian Europe? – that in these sparsely inhabited swamps they were building a hidden slaughter-house for human beings.

We had done about a third of the distance to Cracow when headlights winked and twisted far behind us but fast approaching. The pursuit was bound to overtake us, so there was nothing for it but to give battle, my first battle. I stopped on a narrow bridge for single-line traffic, threw open the rear doors of our truck so that the enemy could see there was no one inside it, and told my four to scatter and take whatever good cover they could find, being careful to keep dry in case we had to enter Cracow on foot.

Left alone, I tried to out-think the enemy. They would naturally assume that we had abandoned our transport on the bridge to delay pursuit, and that we ourselves had got away on foot. They would also assume that our party was unarmed, with a question mark over the SD officer who might be a traitor or might have been killed or kidnapped. In any case the only arm the fugitive possessed was his automatic.

On the right-hand side of the road was a hard shoulder where a vehicle could wait to allow another approaching from the opposite direction to cross the bridge. It was bounded by a bank of raw earth – an obvious point at which to post a piquet which could command the flat stretch of swamp beyond. On the left of the road were only rushes waving gently in the night breeze. A little exploration of the edge would be enough to show that any fugitive must be stuck in the mud and could be collected or used for target practice in the morning if he wasn't drowned meanwhile.

There was no cover on the roadside or the hard shoulder, so I took position on the reverse side of the earth bank. There I was too far from the road to open fire with any chance of success, but I reckoned that orthodox military would never resist the temptation to occupy the bank – though the all-round view from the top would be worthless in the dark – and would choose speed rather than caution.

A vehicle roared up and stopped short of the bridge. It seemed to be a staff car specially adapted for the capture of escapers, for a searchlight was mounted behind the front seat with a light machine-gun below it. Six men jumped out and for a moment stood together in a bunch – proof that they were not expecting any armed opposition. The searchlight was then manned, its beam sweeping the desolate far side of the stream. I couldn't see any of my party, who must have been clinging to the ground in ruts or behind lumps of mud.

Having first satisfied themselves that the truck on the bridge was empty, two men climbed the earth bank as I had foreseen. At a range of twenty feet I was able to kill them cleanly without any trouble. Response was immediate.

Their machine-gunner harmlessly peppered the crest of the bank, the searchlight swept it from end to end and the other two delivered a flank attack, this time with proper care. Meanwhile the bridge was in darkness, allowing me to get away while still remaining in contact. Movements thereafter had to depend on those of the enemy, now reduced to four.

Where the hard shoulder met the stream the slope gave just enough cover to reach the underside of the bridge. The flank attackers were cautiously working their way up the bank and it was safe to crawl round the end of it so long as the two did not look below them. So I ducked under the bridge, clinging to the lattice girder of the steel arch, more afraid of falling in than of the enemy, who must now have passed the bodies of their two comrades and at intervals were loosing off bursts at nothing. The carefully aimed shot seemed to have become unfashionable in modern tactics.

I heard our truck rattling over my head, its headlights shining on the road beyond. With one man lighting up the earth bank and two chasing shadows, only one was left to drive the truck over the bridge and park it clear of the road. A definite objective at last presented itself: to drive on to Cracow in that imposing staff car, provided I remained alive to capture it.

Praying that the searchlight would remain busy, I crept out from under the bridge and padded softly across the open to the back of the truck. The driver had just switched off the engine, and he was at my mercy; but I did not want to fire a shot. My problem was the two on the bank. If they took cover I could never find them in the dark and they were free to attack whenever our party was reunited and vulnerable.

In the event the problem was solved by a mere piece of gangsterism. I stood behind that slaughter-house van, and when the driver left the cab and came abreast of me he had the doubly unnerving experience of seeing an SD officer in dirty uniform and a pistol held at his head – two very good reasons for obeying when I ordered him to keep quiet and turn round. After knocking him out with the butt of his own weapon, I put him in the back of the truck, closed the door and settled down behind the bonnet, waiting for the inexplicable silence of night to have its effect on the others.

I did not have to wait long. The lonely man at the search-light called to his two comrades to return to the car. When they had joined him he drove across the bridge and stopped at the truck. I was unfamiliar with the machine pistol and had been looking for the safety catch. I found it in plenty of time. A nasty, deadly killer at close quarters. They were all three of them in an open car only ten feet away.

I shouted in English and German to summon my companions and at last they appeared, two of them carrying the body of one of the poor devils who had been on the floor of the train. The exertion had been too much for that living substance tortured and twisted by his interrogators and used as a footstool by the guards. I could not think what to do with my prisoner. In those days it went against the grain to kill when I was not immediately threatened. But Broken Face had no doubt. He emptied a magazine into him. Passionate, foolish, understandable hatred. We had some trouble throwing the entire body into the rushes in one piece.

We now had two free uniforms; two more were unwearable and had to go into the marsh with their owners. Broken Face put on one and I took the other, changing my rank from captain to private. Then we drove off to Cracow in a towering thunderstorm which helped to clean up the car. My companions were indifferent to rain and cold and much cheered by some rations which we found in a locker, for they had been given nothing to eat since they started on their journey.

There was at last time to hear their stories. Doubled-Up had been demobilized after the defeat of Poland and then picked up in a raid on his quarter of Cracow and sent straight off to forced labour at Kiel Canal without a chance of communicating with wife or family. Broken Face had been on the same convoy and the same work, and the pair of them, not caring whether they lived or died, had organized a camp mutiny which was betrayed before it got off the ground. They were suspected of being ringleaders and after interrogation were being sent to Auschwitz for, as they supposed, more of it. Man-on-the-Floor, who turned out to be German not Polish, had a different, even sadder story. He was a Jew, a landowner, who had escaped from a concentration camp and been helped and hidden by a good Christian farmer until he was caught. They wanted the name of that decent, civilized man. They hadn't got it. Man-on-the-Floor was proud of that, what was left of him.

It was a help to have two former soldiers in the party. They were familiar with our machine-gun and could also tell me about the use of radio by the military and what we might expect. They agreed that the search party would have called up the unit headquarters as soon as they had closed in on our empty truck, saying that they had started the hunt for the fugitives and would report back as soon as there was any news. Well, there wasn't any, except two pistol shots. That each shot had killed a man would be unknown in the car until the second pair returned from the earth bank, and after that, during the couple of minutes left to them, there was no object in reporting until they knew more exactly what to report.

However, it was certain that posts further down the road would have been alerted as soon as we escaped from Auschwitz station. We had to guess how much they would have been told – probably that four prisoners had seized the truck waiting to take them to camp; that some unknown, possibly a Gestapo officer, must be driving it and that it should be stopped on sight. So should we try to clear the road with our machine-gun or bluff our way through?

Broken Face as always was eager to kill Germans whatever the cost. I doubted if it would be necessary, for there must be normal military traffic on the move to Cracow even at night and we were so obviously military. It was highly unlikely that it would occur to sentries that wretched unarmed prisoners bound for more interrogation and death could have captured our formidable staff car.

I drove while Broken Face, also in Gestapo uniform, sat by my side. The two civilians were huddled against the searchlight mounting hidden under packs and greatcoats. As Broken Face only spoke poor German he was to keep his mouth shut and leave the talking to me. Half of me was confident that we should pass, reassuring the other half which, since waiting is always worse than action, was more jittery than at any other crisis since Stettin.

We had not long to wait before we came to a large notice of HALT, well placed since there was water on both sides of the road and no possible avoidance. As soon as I stopped, a corporal and two of his men came out of a solitary cottage which was serving as a guardroom. I glimpsed inside a comfortable fire and a table with a bottle on it, and hoped that he would not stay out in the pouring rain asking questions or invite death by closely inspecting the car.

'Taking it down to the next post, corporal,' I said. 'They want it in case some escaped prisoners come this way.'

'Waste of time!' he answered. 'They'll never get as far as the town.'

I think he was about to ask us in for a quick nip from the bottle and a warm-up by the fire, so I drove on quickly. It was good news that the next post must be in or very near the city.

It looked as if we should now reach Cracow, but planning was more impossible than ever. Obviously we should have to park the car somewhere and then, unseen by anyone, leave it on foot either in uniform or as civilians. The essential was a safe house where we could change clothes and the victims could recover. Doubled-Up continued to believe that we could find it and that he and Broken Face might manage to acquire new identities. But for me and Man-on-the-Floor, neither of us speaking Polish, the difficulties were formidable. I saw no future as Hauptmann Haase. Wearing a respectable suit I might return to Ernesto Menendez Peraza, provided that only frontier posts had been warned to arrest him and that I could explain his most improbable presence in Cracow.

Dawn was just breaking when we arrived at the outskirts of Cracow. My first impression – and how often they are right! – was of a city in mourning, dominated by its cathedral and castle on the Wavel Hill like a tomb of past glory. It was all dark grey except for an occasional light in a bedroom window. There was not even the usual scatter of early risers in the streets. Twice on seeing our slowly cruising car, pedestrians vanished like rabbits round corners or into gardens, for we were obviously a Gestapo patrol which had picked up some wretched citizen. We had nothing to fear for the moment unless we met some genuine patrol which was bound to greet and question us. We did pass sentries on military establishments but they paid no attention.

There may have been a control post on the main road but, if there was, Doubled-Up's directions enabled us to avoid it. We entered a suburb of deserted factories from which the workers had been seized for slave labour in the Reich and found a quiet spot in a damaged warehouse, where we waited well inside the gate, as if ready to dash out on suspected persons or transport. Morale, influenced by the wasted city, was low. It would not be long before the two privates of the Gestapo had to account for themselves to higher authority. Unfortunately my SD uniform was too muddy and stained to wear and I had no officer's greatcoat to cover it up.

Doubled-Up came out with a proposal which was better than nothing. He insisted that now he could force himself to walk, and that walk he would.

'I shall go to the Great Square,' he said. 'There will be people passing through on their way to work or to the university and I may meet some old friend who will remember how I disappeared. No one is ever allowed back, so he will know I am in trouble.'

Thinking that he would try first to find his family, I wished him luck.

'We have passed my flat already. The house is a billet for troops.'

His expression was and had been set hard. Broken Face tried to comfort him.

'They won't have harmed her. When you were seized you had committed no crime.'

'But when they know our names and how we escaped, they

will try to find her and give her all they would like to give to me. I may be able to find out where she is and warn her but I must never go near her.'

No, it was not to see his lost family that he would walk. His plan was that, about half past eight, we should drive slowly along one side of the square. He would be sitting on a seat, if possible by himself so that no companion could be compromised, and would blow his nose on a white handkerchief if any of us had such a thing – the late Hauptmann Haase had – when we should pick him up quickly. He would then tell us if he had had any success and direct us where to drive.

I asked him what chance there was that the old friend, even if he could be found, would take the risk of helping us.

'There is no man or woman in Cracow who would not,' he replied.

He drew us a rough map of the city and the River Vistula and marked the spot where he would be.

'And till then what do you advise?' I asked him.

He couldn't advise anything. All depended on how long we had before they discovered that we had wiped out the search party and got away in their car. That was hard to guess, but we might well have another hour before radio silence and the car's failure to return began to cause concern. The headquarters would then call up the cottage by the roadside, who would report that the car had gone through on orders from Cracow. Our two ex-soldiers for the first time laughed. Experience had taught them that it would appear a mess of muddled command, typical of any army, to be sorted out after breakfast.

When Doubled-Up had gone, our Jew took me on one side, and said that he was too weak to be of any use to us. I replied with unthinking cheerfulness that if he thought we had no future he should try to find some of his own people to shelter him.

'There are none left in Cracow.'

I was astonished. No one knew better than I the rabid Nazi cruelty in Germany which had dismembered and killed the only love of my past and all my future, but I did not realize that all Jews in conquered Europe were being rounded up, as well as those of the Reich.

'For labour?' I asked.

'Women and children are not much good for heavy labour.'

'Then what are they doing with them all?'

'I only know rumours – terrible rumours.'

I told him I would never leave him till he was in safety or dead. Meanwhile a week in bed, a doctor and good food would make a new man of him.

'But the Poles, sir? They don't much like us either.'

'That was long ago, friend. Now for the Poles everyone who has suffered is a brother.'

We got out of the car and from behind a wall kept watch on the gate of the warehouse, ready for escape on foot if anyone were to show interest in us. Nobody did. Cracow, as I learned later, was now the seat of the German government, and I think it had been swept so clean of workers and possible insurgents that security could be relaxed. After ten minutes Broken Face, always impatient for action, returned to the car and began to examine the mounting of the machine-gun and searchlight. He reported that it was held on only by nuts and bolts, that there was a tool kit on board, and that if we reversed the car round the corner and away from the gate he and I could take the lot off.

So we did it. His regret was evident when we parted from the machine-gun. I pointed out that we still had four machine pistols plus my own handy and accurate little weapon and that if he wanted to die like some ancient hero on a heap of corpses it could easily be arranged. The main question before us was whether we should drive away in our car, now no longer conspicuous, as civilians or as privates of the Gestapo. We decided on the latter, for our party's civilian clothes were too filthy and disreputable. I was to continue driving while Broken Face was to sit in the back guarding our Jew, whose features could hardly be anything but proudly Semitic. Good cover if questioned. We had unearthed one of the last of them.

Dear God, what a city it was when we reached the centre of it! How dared these sewer rats describe the Poles as *Untermenschen* when their ancient capital was one of the flowers of Europe. I was ashamed – so far as I had the odd moment to be ashamed of anything – to have been ignorant of such a seat of learning, its age, beauty and peace comparable to the inner courts of Oxford. The peace now was that of silence, for the professors were in gaol and the students scattered. It was another, wider justification of my attempt on Hitler and those three years as Don Ernesto plotting for a second chance.

The splendid square was a little more animated than any of the streets through which we had passed, though still comparatively empty. A few soldiers were strolling about with cameras. They looked at us and looked away. I detected some disgust, or charitably thought I did. We spotted Doubled-Up and his handkerchief, and when we re-passed him Broken Face leapt from the car and threw him in. He had had enough experience to know every cold and brutal gesture of the Gestapo, and his impersonations must have been convincing for nobody interfered.

Doubled-Up had seen four or five former acquaintances, but only one had recognized him. This friend had sat down next to him showing no sign of welcome and eventually listened to his story as if it were a casual, rather boring conversation with a stranger. Then he had spoken of himself. He had been lucky. He could eat and had a comfortable room. Before the war he was one of the chief municipal engineers. It pleased the invaders' sense of humour to put him in command of a large public urinal. There he had been able to serve his fellow citizens in more ways than one. Through him, members of the underground were able to communicate safely, even to stand next to each other.

Friend did not know enough to tell Doubled-Up where and how we could find safety, but did tell him what our first port of call should be. We should go in civilian dress to a little village near the banks of the Vistula and get in touch with the priest who would warn the partisans of our presence. It was essential to get rid of the car some distance away so that no suspicion could possibly fall on the village.

It all sounded very comforting in theory, but by now our battle at the bridge must surely have been discovered and the number and description of the car signalled to Cracow. On top of that danger we had to cover miles down a main road without any explanation, if stopped, of where we were going. We did not know where prisoners were taken. Our best story was that we were bound for some secret spot where they could be executed. It was weak. In Cracow executions were by no means secret. Doubled-Up's advice was to follow the river and drive fast, so that if any military passing traffic were suspicious we should be well away before they could make up their minds to follow. We could only put our trust in German respect for a uniform. As I had found out, it does not readily occur to them what may be inside it.

Seeing a whole convoy of trucks ahead of us and afraid that we might be challenged as we drove past it, we turned into a side road and found ourselves running through a pleasant district of villas and gardens taken over apparently as billets for high-ranking officers of army and administration. Passers-by, not wishing to tangle with the Gestapo, ignored us, but a colonel of the SD, beautifully polished and uniformed, stepped off the pavement into the road, stopped us and ordered the two miserable privates to get out. I was in two minds whether to run him down or not. Too many eyes might be watching.

Broken Face saluted smartly. I was a little late and took the full blast of abuse. Poor discipline and being improperly dressed. He knew damned well that something was wrong. Either we were joy-riding in an official car on the lookout for women, or we were picking up harmless Poles and black-mailing them into paying up to be set free.

'What did you give these men?' he snapped at Doubled-Up.

'Nothing, sir. I don't know why they wanted me.'

'And you, what's the matter with you?'

Our Jew shrugged his shoulders and held out his hands. The gesture was not typical of him. He was playing the tradi-tional pawnbroker in order that we might have a sure excuse for having detained him.

The officer started to examine the car. While we stood stiffly to attention Broken Face whispered to me in English, 'Turn round! The left, quick!'

I saw what he meant. The brain moves fast when facing certain death, almost as fast as when it snatches back a cut hand to avoid a deeper wound. We had passed the entrance to a little cobbled lane with garages which had once been coach houses on each side of it.

The officer ordered me into the car and jumped in along-side me. An inflexible, intolerable bit of faultless German military he was. He shouldn't have been in the SD at all but commanding a battalion of Prussian Guards. He cannot have approved of Hitler's vulgarity, but likely enough admitted in private that only vulgarity could keep the scum of the Reich at the necessary boiling point.

'Permission to turn round, sir?' I asked.

'Of course, you fool! To Cracow!' he replied, signing his death warrant.

There was no alternative. I swerved into the cobbled lane at such a speed that we nearly overturned. Before the colonel could start whatever he was going to say, Broken Face shot him in the back of the neck.

I was about to throw out the body when Doubled-Up begged me not to. There would be horrifying reprisals against every Polish family in the district, he said. So I dragged the colonel on to the floor in the back, heaved two greatcoats over him and made for the main road. There had been nobody to see us except an old woman. She had looked out of one of the garages at the sound of the shot and seen me dispose of the body. She must have guessed that we were in stolen uniforms, for she blew us a kiss. For long it disturbed me that so sweet a gesture, as if saying goodbye to a grand-child, should accompany the slaughter of a human being, however vile his service.

We had no more trouble on the road, but the nearer we got to our destination the more formidable the difficulties appeared. We had to hide the car. Broken Face and I had to change, as instructed, to civilian clothes. He still had with him his ragged coat and stained trousers, but I seemed doomed to remain a private of the Gestapo or, worse, as Hauptmann Haase. After that we had to make our way to the village on foot and call on the priest. The country was open and though it seemed sparsely inhabited – deserted farms suggested the forced removal of their owners – our movements could be watched, and so it was essential to find a safe place where we could wait till nightfall and then approach the priest. I wished that he had been appointed to some safer parish in the south where I could see the line of the Tatra and the dark mist of forest.

We followed a track very roughly paved with large stones down a tributary stream of the Vistula hoping to find a tall reed bed on fairly solid ground. There was nothing of the sort, and when the track led us past a small patch of woodland on higher ground we chose it for a temporary hiding place, although our presence could not be concealed from a few peasants in distant fields. We were sure they would say nothing and even hoped that somebody might come out with food. It was impossible to get the car right under the trees but an official search of the district was unlikely quite so soon. We outlaws lay down on the soft dead leaves for much-needed rest, myself on the edge of the open to be warmed by the sun.

I must have slept, for I remember suddenly jumping to my feet on hearing shots and equally suddenly dropping flat again as bullets cut into the turf alongside me. I rolled over into cover and watched the development of a skilful attack by a small party of poorly equipped German infantry. However, there was nothing wrong with their short bursts of fire, to which we could not reply because our weapons were in the car. It was all up. I found that I was empty and didn't care very much. I had time to be sorry for my companions who would have preferred to die fighting.

It was our Jew who saved us by simply walking out into the open. The enemy did not attempt to shoot him down and may have been surprised that we continued to hold our fire. He strolled on, upright and fearless, towards a man whose head was sometimes visible behind a patch of nettles; it had no steel helmet and if I could have laid my hands on a weapon with longer range than my pistol he would have been dead.

The man in the nettles, who fortunately understood German, stood up and shouted to his comrades. Five of them there were. It seems incredible that till then Broken Face and I, so tired and so obsessed by mental and physical antagonism to the enemy, had entirely forgotten that we were wearing the enemy's uniform.

Our friends explained that, when they heard that a car with German soldiers and either prisoners or informers had driven to the wood and were isolated from all help and witnesses, the local underground had nipped into their enemy tunics – they were short of boots and breeches – and come out for the kill. They had not been able to understand the lack of resistance and were about to rush us when the only man with any intelligence – we deserved that cut – had the courage to walk out and explain.

When they heard that I was British they were almost reverent, and eager to tell me how everyone understood that when our guarantee to Poland failed to deter the Nazi Reich there was no way we could send troops to help. They supposed I belonged to some suicidal, secret mission and thought it unfair that an officer who could not speak Polish should have been chosen. I did not disillusion them. A secret mission was about right though authorized by no one but myself.

We told them at once that between us we had killed nine of the SD and Gestapo, plus a colonel whose body they would find in the car, and that they must expect all the troops in the garrison to be called out to search for us. With luck it would be assumed that we were still in Cracow and for a day or so the hunt for us might be concentrated there; but we could not count on anything. If the underground were willing to take the risk of helping us, action had to be immediate.

They emptied the car of the weapons, the uniforms and the colonel. For them it was a precious haul. The whole lot was manhandled into the wood and covered up well enough for a casual eye. Final disposal would be carried out after nightfall. Their intention after exterminating the supposed enemy had been to hide their own bits and pieces of German uniforms and arms and then drift away in ones and twos to the fields, returning after dark to bring in the dead and recover their property. They wanted to stick to this plan, taking Broken Face and Doubled-Up with them. Both could be securely hidden until identity documents had been forged for them, when they would be as safe as any other villager – which wasn't saying much.

The Jew and I were a problem out of the ordinary since we could not pass as Poles. It would be best, they thought, if we remained in the wood until they returned with some agreed plan for us, for the car and for the late colonel. Two roving sentries would be on duty to cover the track and the main road and to warn us if there was any danger. We were on no account to try to shoot our way clear, or reprisals on the villages would annihilate this promising section of the underground resistance.

It was after midday when they left, with at least eight hours to go till darkness was deep enough for a party to come out to fetch us. For a while we could blessedly relax in the sun, which already had some power, cheating hunger with two cold baked potatoes and a small flask of vodka, which were all they had. In peace we could listen to a part song of the birds and watch a busy covey of partridges until a peregrine dive-bombed and scattered them. That broke our mood of temporary innocence. We became too conscious of our isolation, of lack of cover on the slopes and the long fields, of the barracks of Cracow emptying into the troop-carriers. That we could remain undiscovered for eight long hours now seemed improbable. We decided that as soon as capture was inevitable we must ensure that we were killed. He had nothing to lose, certain to be whipped off for extermination. Nor had I. But before I died they would require a lot of detailed information from Don Ernesto Menendez Peraza whose passport I still held and intended to hold in case it turned out to be a better safeguard than the pass of Hauptmann Haase in places where neither of them had ever been heard of.

I have continued to call my companion our Jew as if he were some kind of exotic pet because until then names were unimportant in the rush of the escape, and only half heard. I described the three to myself by the nicknames I gave them, with the result that I have forgotten what Doubled-Up and Broken Face were called, but never can I forget Moshe Shapir, my companion in the wood and thereafter.

The first we heard of the return of the partisans was the soft plodding of a pair of horses, approaching over grass. The axles of the haycart they drew were well greased and silent and there was no one with it but the driver. The others joined us quite imperceptibly, materializing from different patches of darkness. Their caution and woodcraft were admirable. And I had always believed the Poles to be impetuous!

Not a light was shown while arms and uniforms were packed under the hay in sacks. The car was extricated and pushed back on to the track by which we had come, while undergrowth was carefully replaced and all tyre marks brushed over. If the wood was still safe, a man would visit it in the morning and perfect the job. I felt that even so my trackers in Africa could have reconstructed all the events of the night, but that was a brilliance denied to Hitler's blasted Aryans and unlikely to be included in any course of Gestapo training.

The party then split up, two going home with the haycart

and four dragging the car along the track by a rope. Two more followed behind with brooms, wiping out the tyre marks wherever they showed on the rough surface of stones. Since Shapir could hardly make any more effort, he was tucked up in the back of the car with his feet – for a change – on the colonel, while I walked alongside the car putting a hand to the wheel when necessary.

Since our scrupulous progress was very slow, two hours had passed before I saw the gleam of the Vistula ahead, I doubted whether they could run the car into the water far enough for it to remain hidden, especially if the enemy suspected what we had done and dragged the river. But again the partisans had thought that one out. A small flat-bottomed barge, shaped like a punt so that the ends, fore and aft, would overhang the slope of the bank – it was probably a country ferry – was waiting for us. On board this barge, which he himself had evidently collected and poled down to the end of the track, was the leader of the band: a tall, powerful man with dark hair and a straight, full moustache, dressed all in black. His eyes were continuously on me, summing up the stranger, but he said little. When he did speak to me it was in French. I was pretty sure that he belonged to the landed gentry, though appearing a peasant like the others.

We shoved the car on board, poled some distance up river, then started it up and let it run off the end into deep water, shipping a lot in the process. The colonel, now naked and suitably weighted, was dropped a good distance away.

When we had run the little barge ashore again, hauling it well up the bank so as to tip most of the water out and leave the bottom boards clear, the leader said to me, 'This has to be your home for the present. I am sorry but it's the best I can do at short notice.'

Sheepskins were laid out for us to lie on and more to cover

us. Food and drink followed. Wading alongside, they pushed the barge up river and through tall reeds, which opened up into a narrow channel. He advised us to draw the barge further into the reeds when the sun rose so that even a plane would be unlikely to spot us.

'It won't hurt this poor devil to lie still for a while,' he added, 'but you will have to have patience. I cannot tell how long before it will be safe to visit you. When it is, I shall come along in a rowing boat.'

'Should I know your name?'

'You may call me Casimir.'

'And our two companions are safe?'

'Warm and well hidden in a roof. I can't get them a doctor for there isn't one nearer than Cracow and his movements are watched. But we can get in touch with him for advice and we have a bone-setter who can carry out whatever treatment he recommends.'

He said that they had wanted to thank me on their knees and they had been so effusive in their praise that he reserved judgement until he himself had met me.

'Now is there anything I can do for you while you are here?'

'Nothing. All I want is to have the captain's uniform brushed and thoroughly cleaned. I daren't use the colonel's.'

'Our central command can often communicate with London. If you have a wife and family, would you like her to be told that you are alive and well?'

'I have no wife. I would have had if Hitler had not tortured and killed her.'

'In my case it was my daughter.'

'Then Lord help the Nazi who falls into your hands.'

'I was just about to say the same to you,' he answered.

We were left alone among the frogs and that mysterious

waving of rushes by no apparent body which always fills the watcher with a vague unease, though knowing that it is caused not by the passage of Pan searching for a hollow reed but a fish or eel among the roots. The east began to lighten and the silence of still water was broken by the clamour of duck setting out on the morning flight, great arrowheads of winged life and purpose.

Arms round my knees, I sat up in the bows, sure of my own purpose but wondering what my destination should be whenever I was free to choose. Till then I had been wholly engaged in avoiding the ever-present destination of death. It was obviously essential to get out of Poland, where every officer of the SD and Gestapo would be on the lookout for their bogus colleague. All routes to the east led through concentrations of the military and ultimately to the Russian front. To the west was Germany again. So it had to be south over the Tatra, provided that the partisans could recommend safe paths. What conditions I would find on the other side of the Carpathians in Slovakia were beyond guessing. The poor Slovaks, once a contented people of the empire and then an unenthusiastic partner in Czechoslovakia, were probably pro-German.

Moshe Shapir, who had been sleeping his way back to some remnant of health, woke up. He said that it was the most memorable luxury of his life to feel warm again. Recalling my own sensations after I had emerged from my Dorset burrow and wrapped myself in von Lauen's fleece-lined coat, I was inclined to agree with him.

I asked him if he had any plans for his future, assuming we had one.

'Of course,' he answered. 'I shall go to Palestine.'

It seemed worlds away and no more than a compass bearing. The route must lead through Turkey, a truly neutral country where I might be accepted by my countrymen, though I had little hope of it after my experience in Sweden. But to hell with neutral countries! More tempting was the thought of Greece, conquered and occupied, where I spoke a recognizable version of the language and might intensify my personal war up to its end.

The duck settled and the day passed. A plane flew low down the Vistula, possibly searching for any sign of us but unlikely, we decided, to have spotted the barge. We had bent reeds partly over it and concealed ourselves and everything of unnaturally light colour beneath them. More alarming was the distant sound of a heavy vehicle passing along the track beside the wood.

Around midnight we heard the splash of oars and the rustle of a boat being pulled through the rushes. The dark, grim Casimir came alongside with more food and drink and some temporary comfort. He told us that a search party had indeed come down the track as far as the water's edge and found nothing. They had visited his village but left after asking a few questions, sure of its innocence because the Gestapo had its own informer there. I said that I wondered he had not met with a fatal accident.

'That would be suicide.'

'It's you?'

'Yes. I am a favourite in Cracow. I am a simple squire, as I think you call it in English, poor and ambitious and not such a patriot as the great men and the peasants. I am a good Aryan and I detest the miserable Slavs and communists and Jews. God, how easy it is to babble their nonsense!'

Fortunately Moshe did not understand French. He was in no mood to appreciate irony.

'I know. I have done the same I said. 'We Nazis are the salt of the earth and the hope of Europe.'

He slapped me on the back and laughed. It was the laughter of a soul in hell, quite joyful considering the flames.

I asked him what were the chances of a successful escape into Slovakia. He replied that the passes were heavily guarded and whatever we pretended to be we should not get through.

'Unless you can bluff your way over in that uniform,' he added. 'We have had it thoroughly cleaned for you. Beautiful boots, friend. Beautiful boots to kick with.'

I told him that the risk was too great. It was a delightful thought that all security officers of the Reich for miles around would have their identities checked and re-checked when passing through any control, but it meant that I could not pretend to be Haase with a photograph that was no likeness. I would wear his boots and keep his pistol and documents but abandon his uniform, which was too bulky anyway to be carried on my back.

'What else have you?'

'A Nicaraguan passport in the name of Ernesto Menendez Peraza. Anyone who is caught with that will be taken straight to Hitler's headquarters for treatment. Ernesto only died four days ago, so they won't have taken him off the blacklist yet. No, I must use the skills of a hunter. Arms, not bluff. And I am sure of myself in mountain and forest.'

'You can't avoid the tops,' he said, 'and you'll find them very bare and closely watched. They mean to keep their Polish slaves where they belong. Judging by what your two friends say of you, you're as cunning as a lynx and deadly as rabies, but you can't travel with one of those machine pistols slung on you.'

'I'll leave you those. Can you give me a rifle in exchange and a screwdriver?'

'What do you want the screwdriver for?'

'So that I can carry it in two parts, down my trousers or under my shirt.'

He thought this over. His face – what I could see of it in the dark – showed a reluctance and then cleared.

'I will give you my father's Mannlicher. She dates back to 1908, but the old lady is accurate at five hundred metres and more if you love and cherish her and find out her little ways. I bought fresh ammunition just before the war and tested it.'

Feeling that he was making a great sacrifice, I said it was noble of him and asked what his father used it for.

'You won't have heard of the Rifle Association. That was our answer to the Russia of the Tsars – a hundred and seventy Poles who crossed the frontier from the Habsburg empire and attacked.'

'Well, I suppose she won't mind if it's Germans now.'

'She won't mind if you are behind her, my man. Now sleep as much as you can, for we shall move at night. And you had better leave this poor chap in my charge. He'll hold you back.'

'I have promised that I won't desert him.'

'But how far can he walk?'

I translated the question to Moshe.

'I will lift up mine eyes to the hills from whence cometh my help,' he answered.

It sounds mysteriously better in English than in German. I think of David's raiding party pinned down by the Philistines in the coastal plain and crying to his God for reinforcements from Jerusalem. A poem of all eternity, yet on its day, I suppose, only the passionate appeal of an over-bold commander.

'He believes he can climb anything on his way to Palestine.'

'I'll tell that to our priest.'

'The one we were told to call on? He won't mind helping?'

'Are you forgetting that in spite of all we are still Christians?

Now, if only Mr Shapir could ride, the priest and I would have a plan for you.'

'If it has four legs I can ride it,' Moshe replied when I translated this for him.

I had thought that his light, lean body was wholly due to pain and starvation. His answer made me look at him again. The muscles were wasted, the face fallen in, but even when well fed that body had been lean.

'A jockey?'

'A trainer and successful. I was foolish enough to believe that would make them forget I was a dirty Jew – so long as the racing tips I gave the Gauleiter were profitable. And then I had a wonder two-year-old. I told him to back it both ways for as much as he could afford. Need I tell you that it lost and badly? These things happen. Next day I was arrested and my stable confiscated.'

'And if he had been a Prussian gentleman of the old school, he'd have shed a tear with you over the second bottle,' Casimir exclaimed. 'What swine they give power to! No wonder the rest are rotten with fear!'

He now seemed very confident, but disappointed us by saying that we must wait a night or two more as he needed a permit and had to collect the horses. He would explain it all later. There was no hope of riding across the frontier into Slovakia but before we had to take to our feet we should be deep in the forests of the Tatra.

Another night and two more days we had to spend among the reeds. We found that we were not impatient to leave. The peace of sky and birds and water was sinking into us, creating an illusion of safety. This was a home to which we had come – I after the carnage of that journey from Stettin, he after such despair that he had asked to be allowed to die. He was now noticeably recovering. At first he would walk if he had to but, if he didn't have to, he preferred to crawl. He could even laugh at himself as Moses in the bulrushes when we washed in the icy Vistula, warming ourselves afterwards with the blessed sheepskins outside and vodka within.

When we were not sleeping or sharing the silence of the river, we discussed the question of what we should do once out of Poland. The map in our memories was quite unable to keep up with the reality of the new frontiers of 1938 and 1939, but the problem was eased by German victories; there were no more Russians to complicate matters for 1500 miles to the east, and in the Tatra region of the Carpathians, Slovakia, Hungary and Romania must, it seemed to us, all meet at a crossroads. All three were politely called independent, which presumably meant that they had their own frontier guards opposite German posts. Any of the lot would gladly arrest us.

Towards the end of a long night Casimir arrived with a threadbare suit of civilian clothes for me. Two of his partisans took our barge back to wherever it belonged, after landing us on a clean bank of grass, where we found four horses saddled and waiting. To my surprise they were not the rough, sturdy animals of the Polish countryside but cavalry chargers. Didn't Casimir think that we should be too conspicuous?

'You may well ask,' he replied. 'They belonged to two squadrons of our cavalry which rode into Hungary after our defeat and were interned. Recently four officers escaped, stole these horses and rode for home. A mistake. They were better off in the internment camp. They didn't realize what the Nazis have done to us.

'When they arrived they said that the Hungarians had treated them well and that it was a matter of honour to return the horses. At Cracow the governor-general refused. He said that the Poles were serfs and had no honour, but the military commander who hadn't heard the word honour for years was amused and insisted that the escaped prisoners were right. He couldn't detail soldiers to take the horses back without the hell of a row, so he decided to have it done discreetly by reliable Poles. That's us. And we have all the scraps of paper to take the horses to the frontier. When I asked how we should get back, I was told to walk.'

We had to lift Moshe into the saddle but once he was there I recognized that he and his horse were one living thing. We then set out across the open fields in single file, riding slowly in order to cross the main road in full daylight and avoid suspicion. Even so, we were stopped by a patrol, to which Casimir, leading the spare horse, submitted his permits with proper humility. We two were Slovaks who didn't speak a word of Polish or German and looked the part huddled in our sheepskin coats and unshaven and squalid. The patrol commander made his men laugh by saying he hoped our permits covered our lice as well.

Soon we were in the foothills of the Tatra. On the flanks of the wide valley up which we rode, agriculture gave place to forest. The slopes steepened. It was becoming country in which I could avoid capture indefinitely given a supply of food, but I could not see how Moshe would ever be able to climb out of the valleys when we were left on our own. I drew up alongside Casimir to ask him if he had any plans. He said that it depended how things were at the frontier. We would see.

'You were right to leave that uniform behind,' he said. 'I have found out more about you from my contact. He wants me to keep an eye open for communist agents. Fool! We are all Poles.'

The Gestapo, he gathered, were sure that I was in Cracow or nearby. The four men I had rescued were of no importance and so I must have been trying to escape in any way I could and without any definite plan. I might be a Russian prisoner-of-war from north Germany and have stolen a uniform in the camp.

That was satisfactory. It suggested that they were still looking for the body of Haase and did not know that Don Ernesto was alive. But there was no time to waste. It could not be long before someone in the Sicherheitsdienst put two and two together.

Up through broad-leaved forest we went to the pines on the narrow summit of the ridges, then down again to oak and beech and grass. The country was a miniature of that herring-bone of valleys which drop down from the cordillera of the Andes to the plain of the Amazon, but here at least were paths manageable for our horses in single file. They and we had had more than enough of it when we came down into the valley of the young River Dunajec, where the hush of the forest floor changed to the chatter of fast streams and the beat of falls as the water poured down from the side ravines.

We had covered some thirty miles when we came to the junction of the Dunajec and a considerable tributary. Between the two was a peninsula bounded as if it were sea shore by a tumble of rocks and here and there sharp little cliffs. Willows overhung the rocks concealing the interior. Casimir turned off the track and forded the Dunajec, then rode round the point to the other side where, shadowed by the forest, was a path leading inland.

We came out of the screen to a long, lush meadow with a donkey, a cow and some geese on it. At one end was a solid hut of rough timber and a small kitchen garden. The owner of this hidden paradise came out to meet us, long-haired and wearing a black robe which was vaguely ecclesiastical. He embraced Casimir, who was evidently an old friend, and when we had been lengthily introduced addressed me in a sort of

English and Moshe in excellent Hebrew – at least Moshe thought it was, having himself only enough Hebrew to say the formal prayers.

While we were unsaddling the horses and turning them loose in the meadow, Casimir told me that our host had been a Catholic priest who had been unfrocked for heresy and become a hermit, deciding that from then on he would commune with his Maker without outside interference. I sympathized, being myself at bottom a sort of deadly hermit. If not for my self-imposed duty to take arms against Hitler, I could have lived happily and alone in that hermitage between the waters, unknown to all my fellows except the rare forester clinging to the steep and pathless slopes of the valley.

It was Casimir's plan that we should camp there for the night and in the morning he would take the horses on to the frontier alone.

'Won't they expect us to be with you?' I asked.

'Not necessarily. I might have started out alone. But in case the road patrol has reported that there were three of us, I shall tell them that one of you was badly thrown and the other stayed to look after him.'

'And when you return?'

'Your next move depends on what I find up there. Wait and we will see.'

He was off at dawn, leading one horse as before and driving the other two in front of him – simple enough since the precipitous mountain forest fenced both sides of the track. He left his father's rifle with me, saying that, although he had special permission to carry it into the Tatra, any officer up there who wanted to relieve boredom by going out after deer would not hesitate to confiscate it.

Meanwhile we spent with our host a day of memorable peace. Like any good village priest, he had some knowledge of herbs and simple medicine and played the good Samaritan with Moshe, whose health and colour seemed to respond – owing more to the human love, I think, than to the ministrations. An odd fellow, that hermit! I do not know in what his fearsome heresy consisted, but it was worthy of imitation. Though we had no common language, speech seemed unnecessary. His animals, too, showed marked affection for all human beings, having only this gentle soul by which to judge us. When I bathed in the river, Wanda the donkey accompanied me, while cow and geese lined up and watched approvingly like a party of non-swimmers on a beach.

Casimir came home in the evening, having made fast time, for it was downhill all the way. He reported that there were Germans on the Polish side of the frontier and that their posts were well placed and very difficult to avoid. He advised trying a rough path which would lead us out of the valley of the Dunajec, across another valley and ridge and then on to the bare uplands above the tree-line.

Such a journey was impossible for Moshe. Yet it was pointless to remain in the hermit's paradise and, hidden though it was, far too dangerous for him. I suggested that perhaps I could buy the donkey, for I had not used any of my German marks since Stettin.

Casimir went with me to open negotiations. Our host flatly refused to sell Wanda, saying that she was like a daughter to him in his loneliness: but, since our need was indeed great, both would go with us until we were near the frontier and ready to cross.

That I could not allow. I asked Casimir to tell him that we might be shot on sight and certainly would be if captured. He and Wanda, our accomplices, must expect to share the same fate.

There was more conversation between the two. I could see

that the hermit was insisting on some plan and that Casimir was trying to dissuade him.

'He says that there can be no danger in the thick forest, so he and Wanda will go with you as far as the tree-line and set you on a route which will take you down into Slovakia without any more climbing.'

In the morning we regretfully said goodbye to our saviour Casimir. He had left his people alone too long and was always afraid of some too impetuous action in his absence like their attack on the wood. The most troublesome duty of a leader of partisans was, he said, to prevent premature adventures which could lead to penetration of the cell. Any indiscretion could be fatal to all of them if the presence of Doubled-Up and Broken Face in the village together with the uniforms and arms were discovered. I can only hope that his instinct for survival in the midst of German and then Russian armies carried his courageous little cell safely through to the Poland they served.

We set off along the banks of the tributary valley and then tackled the steepest of all forests we had met, where there were no obvious paths but only barren gaps between trees, each clinging to its pocket of soil. Wanda dictated how we should proceed. She had a light load of our sheepskins and food for a couple of days but refused to carry Moshe on her back as well, though our hermit spoke severely into one long and obstinate ear, while I reminded her that in Mediterranean lands donkeys as small as she would carry some massive grandmother and her full basket. However, she had no objection to towing Moshe at the end of a rope, taking three of her delicate steps to one stumbling stride of his.

At rest in the paradise I had not seriously tested the hermit's mutilated version of English. His eyes and hands were alone capable of communicating whatever was necessary. But in unexpected emergencies speech is essential and I found that if I spoke slowly he could understand me very well, but could not reply. He then tried Latin on me, and the position was reversed. I could understand him but, in spite of a classical education from the age of nine, I could not reply. One might think teachers believed that citizens of the Roman empire only communicated with each other in writing.

Down into another valley we went and up another ridge. The narrow top was all rock and pines and led gently downhill. The hermit said that the frontier straddled the ridge and was somewhere below us. He proposed that we should leave Moshe and Wanda to rest and eat while he and I went ahead to detect the guard post, if any, and settle on a route which could be easily found and followed at night. I refused to hear of it. I would go out alone and when I returned he and Wanda must make for home at once.

The first sign of the frontier was a wooden watchtower, unexpected in such remoteness. Evidently the hermit's knowledge of the borderland was out of date; the summit of the ridge, with its fairly open forest and silent, easy going over the pine needles, must have been a favourite route for illicit travellers between Poland and Slovakia. Trees had been cut down along the line, so that I could get a good view of the post from the edge of the remaining cover. There was a guard close to the watchtower and barbed wire – an impassable roll of it – closing the approach. My first thought was that the enemy could have chosen a better spot for the barrier, since it seemed unlikely that the wire ran all the way down to the valleys on the east and west sides of the ridge. Any enterprising fugitive ought to be able to find a way round it.

I started by exploring the promising western side, which was below the watchtower's line of sight. The trees had not been cleared and the wire disappeared into them. In case the engineer of the SD had been more professional than I thought, I approached very cautiously and found that the wire ended at the edge of a precipice, and a crumbling edge at that. So I went back and tried the eastern side. This was too bare and steep for all but a scatter of trees. A network of goat paths ran between the rocks, here and there blocked by wire. I suspected that anyone who confidently avoided the obstruction would have his foot blown to bits, or at least set off an alarm. The guards were bound to get their man, especially if there were a searchlight on the watchtower to help.

I turned back into the safety of the pines and was about to rejoin my companions and report that this route offered little hope of getting across into Slovakia, when a party of five men, bristling with arms, set out from the guard house for an evening patrol. Some of them were at the mercy of the Mannlicher slung on my back, but that would do us no good. The consequent alert all along the Polish side of the frontier would mean that we should walk into trouble at easier crossings where the guards might otherwise be taking their duties less seriously.

Dusk was falling as the patrol did a short round of that difficult east side. When they failed to flush any Poles or partridges from the shelter of the rocks, they filed off into the forest on the summit of the ridge, going out along the eastern side and certain afterwards to search the west. If I had been alone there, they could search as long as they liked, but they could not miss the group of two men and a donkey even if Wanda kept her mouth shut. That was improbable, for she liked to welcome the stranger.

Action of some sort I had to take. I thought of allowing them to be arrested and attacking as they were brought back to the guard house. But would they be brought back? One was a Pole and the other a Jew, both expendable on the spot. Then I thought of giving the patrol more sporting game to hunt, but if I got away it would only be a temporary help to the others. I remember wondering what was on the other side of the frontier and whether Slovaks, in the improbable event of wanting to slip into Poland, would have the same trouble at that post which I had conceitedly judged to be badly placed.

Slovaks trying to cross. Well, it was worth a try. Even if I fell and was killed, the excitement at the post and the recall of the patrol should give the hermit and Moshe time to get away. In the fading light I took another look at that cliff on the western side. The roll of wire was hanging over the edge, so was a large chunk of cliff top, which indeed was stopped from falling only by the wire itself. It was just possible to follow the cleft under the wire, provided I pushed the rifle in front of me.

Wriggling on elbows and toes, I played the rabbit. At any rate I did not make a sound. Earth and pebbles dislodged fell into the tapering bottom of the cleft. The worst moment was when the back of my coat caught on the barbed wire. No backward wriggle would free it. I had to adopt the antics of a guru without muscles in order to get my hands behind my back and tear each barb separately out of the cloth.

The far end of the cleft opened on to blank nothing without a handhold, but there the Mannlicher helped. Asking silent pardon of Casimir's father, I reached up and dug the barrel into a crack. With a toe-hold on the wire itself, that allowed me to pull myself up into Slovakia. I cleaned the barrel with a stick as well as might be and squinted along it. No damage. That was as well, for I intended the rifle to provide the diversion necessary to keep that patrol away from Moshe and the hermit.

The belt of tree stumps was narrower on this side of the frontier, and it was simple in the dusk to crawl through to better cover. There I waited until the searchlight began to throw a beam down the eastern side and then for good measure played on the trees behind me. I shot it out. High and right, I guessed, but it was difficult to tell. I loosed off two more rounds into the watchtower, of which one, ripping through the planks, struck another target, for I heard a howl of agony. A nasty wound it would be if the bullet had turned on a nail.

The only thing now was to be ready in the darkness for any chance the gods might offer. The guard house erupted. A Verey light went up, showing them nothing but burning long enough for me to see that the guards had split up and were going to attack from both sides of the ridge. There were few of them to do it and I reckoned that every man left in the place must be engaged. In their commendable dash they had left the gate open. Under the circumstances the safest place, offering escape from encirclement as well as easy return to Poland, was the garrison.

I fired one more shot to encourage them to continue their search of the forest and ran for the guard house. I had trouble in finding the gate on the Polish side through which the earlier patrol had set out, and had just got my hand on it when I heard them doubling back to take part in whatever night operation was going on. A garbage can stood by the gate ready for emptying down the hill in the morning. I crouched behind it. Looking back, I think that was the most outrageous gamble which I took. Only one of them had to look round and give me a burst from his automatic, but I was prepared to bet that in their hurry to reinforce their comrades none of them would. One of them, after running a few yards,

75

did turn back to shut the gate but by that time I was outside it and lying flat.

I found my party completely unaware that a patrol had been anywhere near them, and of course alarmed by my long absence and the sound of shots coming from the darkness where the frontier must be. Moshe, who knew me best, was certain that I would not have crossed and gone on alone, but that I might well be dead. The hermit, inspired by Casimir's exaggerations, thought that if any killing had been done I had done it. They had decided to wait for me till first light and meanwhile to drop down a little from the top of the ridge into thicker cover.

That move was a disaster. The hermit had sprained an ankle stepping on a stone which had rolled away under his foot. He blamed himself and couldn't think what to do for us since he was no more use as a guide. Hugging the poor ankle, he said – at least I thought he said, 'Age! Age! And once I was as sure-footed as a goat.'

To be landed with two cripples was a reminder that luck cannot last for ever. His intention was to slide down the slope from tree to tree until he reached the bottom of the valley and the track that we had quickly crossed. There he would stop and bathe the ankle in a stream. Eventually some peasant with a cart might pass; if not, he would hobble on to a village where he was known.

'And I shall leave Wanda with you,' he said.

I protested that we could not deprive him of his little animal, who, he had said, was dear to him as a daughter. He replied that she could not dive directly down the slope and that he was incapable of walking down in the long zigzags by which we had climbed to the summit of the ridge. Certainly it was near impossible on one leg without long and painful rests, and he would be unable to escape or to account for himself by any credible story if the guards decided to investigate the Polish side of the frontier. All the same, I think that from a sense of guilt he exaggerated the problem.

'No, you must take her,' he insisted. 'Moshe's need is greater than mine.'

He was sure that, since this old smugglers' route had been blocked, the regular valley passes would be controlled even more tightly. He thought we ought to aim for the plateau where Moshe could easily manage short marches over the turf and we could see trouble from far off before we walked into it. The best plan – short of going back into the foothills, civilization and roads alive with military – was to drop down into the eastern valley, cross another ridge and valley and then strike up a fairly easy escarpment until we came out of the forest on to the uplands where we should meet only shepherds. Without Wanda Moshe would never do it.

'I could tow him or carry him myself.'

'Not for long, strong though you are. And you have seen how Wanda can sense the easiest path.'

'But how can we ever return her to you?'

'I have thought of a way.'

It was difficult to get from him exact spoken directions, but with two fingers he drew a map in the pine needles which, as he patted the furrows into shape, turned out to be an intelligible relief map. After questions in English and answers in Latin, I had a clear picture of what he proposed. When we had crossed the next ridge and valley and had completed what he called an easy climb, we were to go eastwards until the Peak of Dukla came in sight. We should then see a church tower rising from the trees not far below us. The priest's house was on our side of it, the last house in the village. At the side of the house was a walled paddock, probably with a few sheep in it.

'The priest is an old friend who has never condemned me. Leave Wanda with him. He knows her and will recognize her. In a few days I will borrow a horse and cart and go out to fetch her home. When you are back on the upland, circle round Dukla. All is then downhill, and with God's help you will arrive in Slovakia.'

It was wisest for all of us to get off the ridge at once. To the hermit, darkness made little difference. He could continue sliding and creeping like a lizard over the dead leaves, with gravity doing all the work, until he arrived at the bottom. He said an affectionate goodbye to Wanda, who wanted to follow him but could not face a slope where her tail was so much higher than her head. We assured both of them that we would see they were reunited – I say both, because by this time we knew Wanda capable of such human devotion that it was mere prejudice to deny her some human understanding. Her velvet nose sought comfort from Moshe, to whom she had become attached by more than the rope between them.

We crossed the ridge to its eastern side and then felt our way down through the pines, very slowly traversing the slope until we came to a flat terrace where the darkness was darker than the night, indicating thick cover overhead. There we ate the last of our food supply and slept a little, while waiting for enough light to be able to choose a path down to the bottom of the valley. On arrival we spent the rest of the day by the stream, Moshe cuddling the soft green turf, Wanda cropping it around him and I wandering in search of game.

The hermit and his pine needles had given us unmistakable directions for continuing our march to the east. The next ridge took us a full day to climb and descend, with of course frequent stops for Moshe and Wanda. Next morning we started on the easy march up through the dappled world of the broad-leaved forest. East it was, but pathless and seemingly endless, except perhaps to Wanda who plucked and chewed while walking. Where the pines began I spotted a young roebuck, which evidently had never seen a donkey before and stayed a second too long to satisfy curiosity. I grilled the steaks and chops, setting aside the latter for next day. I had to warn Moshe, who hadn't tasted meat for over a year, to go easy. He slept fitfully but woke clear-eyed. Our mountain sanatorium was doing him a world of good and helpless collapse was growing rare.

At dawn we left the forest below and came out on to a rolling plateau which reminded me of my beloved English downland though six times as high and still with pockets of snow where sun could not reach the drifts. After the security of the trees, I felt exposed in this no-man's land, but the hermit had been right; we never met a soul. If we were observed, the observer was as anxious to keep out of the way as we were. There were signs of fighting, which seemed from scraps of uniform and ironmongery to date from the last stand of fragmentary Polish troops in 1939, rather than the retreat of the Russians two years later. Searching the waves of highland to identify the Dukla Peak some twenty miles or so distant, I caught a quick glimpse of horsemen quickly disappearing over a skyline.

In the early afternoon we saw the little bell tower of a church poling up from the trees and hoped it was the right one. After another mile, we came to a wide beaten track crossing the range and dipping into the black woods. I left Moshe and Wanda in the cover of a cluster of rocks and went down to see if there was a house and paddock which fitted the hermit's description. There was, and better still a narrow path by which we could lead Wanda down under cover of darkness without taking the track or disturbing the villagers. We had to be cautious, for I heard two voices singing in

German with more heartiness than tempo. A tavern probably. Fraternization could be ruled out. The frontier must be near enough for guards off duty to slip down to the village and flaunt their superiority over sullen peasants who, for the sake of their families and houses, dared not kill them.

Since the songsters might at any time decide to return to their post, I could not show myself in the open; so I lay under the trees by the side of the track and waited. Soon afterwards two German infantrymen well primed with vodka passed me on the track, and when they were safely out of sight over the brow of the hill I made for the rocks where I had left Moshe and Wanda. They were not there.

Moshe came running up from behind the scattered iron bones of a burned-out truck among which he had hidden, and quickly explained. He had let Wanda graze freely and she had wandered off towards the track where the two soldiers had spotted her. Unarmed there was nothing he could do, and guessing that they would search the rocks for the owner of the donkey, and pull him in for questioning, he had very wisely crawled into the debris of the truck. Since all Poland belonged to them, the soldiers had seen no reason why they should not acquire an abandoned donkey, even though her owner might merely be drinking in the village. They were still in sight. I regret to record that Wanda was giving them no trouble. It may be that they were kinder to animals than to the conquered.

I had promised to deliver Wanda safely and that had to be done. Without time to work out the consequences, I could only vaguely foresee a mist of problems, ranging from the difficulty of stalking those arrogant marauders over open ground to our defencelessness against any punitive expedition and possible reprisal on the village. They were now the best part of a mile ahead but casually strolling along.

A shallow dry valley running roughly parallel to the track gave me a chance of catching up. Racing along it, I found that the track swung left across the depression, so that the party would be nicely lined up for me. But the range was too long. I could not kill them both without the risk of hitting Wanda. And both it had to be. If there were a survivor, he could tuck himself in behind a rock with his automatic and could not be stalked or rushed.

I took the risk that when they were at the bottom of the dip they would not be able to see anyone running into position on the far side. It took good timing to manage this and I was panting so hard when I dropped flat that I feared I couldn't hit a haystack. But either I had run faster than I thought possible or they had stopped for an instant to light a cigarette out of the wind. As soon as the first head and shoulder appeared, with Wanda still behind the edge, I killed with the second shot – second because I had forgotten that the Mannlicher should be aimed a trifle low and left. The next head quickly and properly vanished behind waving grass on the lip of the depression. He could see me and gave me a burst from his Schmeisser, which at that range was optimistic.

I dashed off a little further, twisting like a snipe, and lay down to think. My opponent vanished. I could not tell whether he had slipped down the slope and was running for his life or whether he was crawling along just below the edge to close the range. Wanda's movements were no help at all. She had bolted back to the opposite side of the dip and was quietly grazing.

He soon left me in no doubt what he had done, bobbing up and down and squirting the position where he believed me to be – and he wasn't far wrong – with his blasted hosepipe. I didn't dare to show anything of myself above the grass. He had seen some fighting, this man. It looked like stalemate until dusk, when one of us would attack, and succeed or not.

I saw that Wanda had stopped grazing and was interested in something out of my sight. When the object stood up and quickly crouched again, it turned out to be Moshe. Having had a clear view of both of us, he realized that we were unlikely to take our eyes off each other for a moment and walked with astonishing courage quietly down into the dip where I lost sight of him. I provided some covering fire, which was returned with interest. Then to my horror there was another burst which was not aimed in my direction. Moshe walked calmly over the edge. Thank God the bit of head which first appeared was bare, dark-haired and recognizable just in time.

'You can get up,' he said. 'That was me.'

He had silently taken the Schmeisser from the dead guard. He explained that he knew how to use it because he had watched me.

We had a look at the body. The nape of the neck had been blown clear away. A cleaner wound would have been a kinder initiation.

'I have killed a man. God forgive me! I thought I was above vengeance.'

I assured him that it was not vengeance, that he had risked his life to save a friend.

'Then it should have been my own death, not that of another.'

That called for a lecture to my very promising pupil.

'Moshe, you want to reach Palestine, or Israel as you call it. To settle your people there has meant war with the Arabs for us. To stay there will mean war for you. How about Joshua, David and Co.?'

He did not attempt an answer. We recovered Wanda and sat down to discuss how on earth to get rid of bodies on open grassland without a spade. That was our obvious duty for the sake of the hermit's friend, his church and his village.

With the Mannlicher and one of those machine pistols, I was now well armed for long or close distances. Moshe was unwilling to pick up the other until I pointed out that he was under no obligation to use it and that when slung with arms like a Balkan bandit I could neither move freely nor fire any one of them without delay.

For the time being we left the dead where they were and led Wanda back to the shelter of the rocks to wait for sunset. When the green of the plateau had turned to dark grey, we entered the trees by the path I had found and passed round the stone wall of the paddock. No sheep were inside. It looked as if the priest had turned his pocket of land into a kitchen garden. He would start his morning with a strong prejudice against Wanda if he found his spring cabbages eaten up, but for our own sakes we could not call on him and let him know that she was there. Moshe solved this absurd problem, remembering that when the hermit gave her a gentle wallop behind – which we had never presumed to do – she would bray in protest; so as soon as we had opened the gate he gave her a deserved hug and kiss And then destroyed romance. The resulting bray from the direction of his house and garden could be heard by the priest wherever he was.

We made for the open downs, following the track for the sake of speed and Moshe's failing legs. At the edge of the tree-line, we dived for cover, for we had been fiercely and unmistakably challenged in Polish. I replied in French and English saying that we were fugitives from Cracow. A horseman crashed through the undergrowth towards us while another threw light on us. Finding that we did not understand Polish, he gestured to us to come out with our hands behind our heads. We were marched off into the open, where I saw a shadowy group of four more mounted men and a baggage horse carrying a light machine-gun.

The commander of this band demanded in German – good Viennese German of the old empire – to know our names and our business, I told him that we were trying to cross into Slovakia and that for the present we thought it best to have no names. Then why had we left behind a hee-hawing donkey which could arouse all the Tatra? I replied with another question: had he ever heard of a certain man named Casimir?

At once the atmosphere of suspicion was changed. I was allowed to explain the presence of Wanda in a district where apparently there was no other donkey and that we had been told to deliver her to the priest. There had, however, been a small incident en route and I hoped he could tell us how to get rid of two German bodies so that their disappearance would remain a mystery.

'That was the firing we heard?'

'That was the firing you heard. And if the frontier post is anywhere near they will have heard it too. So be careful!'

'They won't turn out in force till daylight. Shots in the night are nothing new and this lot value their skins. Now come with us!'

'My companion is still recovering from what the Gestapo did to him,' I said, 'and he must not walk any more. Have you a spare horse?'

He himself immediately dismounted and helped Moshe into the saddle.

'Now lead us to the bodies!'

'We have only to follow the track. Where it turns left into the dip we shall find them.'

We walked together behind the horses. When I let him know that I was English, he asked me how I came to speak German so well.

'My mother was Austrian and I often visited her parents.'

'Where?'

'Not far from Uzhgorod in Slovakia. Down below us they lived on what was left of their estate.'

'I can take you there.'

'Not now. Not any more.'

We picked up the bodies, tying each down behind a rider, and marched a few miles to the east, where again we entered the forest and arrived at what seemed a temporary bivouac cunningly placed on the edge of a gorge which could not be seen at all from the high tops, and would appear to an observer on the opposite side of the valley merely a terrace of the cliff wide enough to support a mixture of beech and pine. Here were a dozen more partisans with plenty of food and ammunition and another light machine-gun. They could not risk a fire but otherwise seemed to be carefree and at home.

I asked if they were all Poles.

'No, my friend. We represent the provinces of the vanished empire. Here are Poles, Slovaks, a Czech, two Romanians from the Bucovina and myself, an Austrian. I represent, in all but its hopeless inefficiency, imperial Vienna, when at least we remained Europeans and men of honour. For me as for my ancestors frontiers are only a nuisance.'

He delighted in his irony, reminding me of all the smash-and-grab since March 1939. The Czechs were swallowed by Hitler. Slovakia timidly put itself under his protection. Poland and Hungary collected a common frontier from the garbage, and after the defeat of Poland Russia took her slice of Poland and in 1940 annexed Bessarabia and Bucovina from Romania.

'And now the Russians are back on the Volga and the frontiers are a spider's web of abandoned posts and wire. No one knows them as we do, not even the garrison commanders.'

'What are your objectives?'

'Simple. To squash these lice who crawl over honour and humanity. If you care to join us I will welcome a Jew who, I can see, remains a fine horseman in spite of the Gestapo and an Englishman who has the national virtue of gnawing the enemy while keeping his mouth shut.'

I could see no point in keeping my mouth shut any longer, so I gave him my history since the escape from Rostock without mentioning how I got there. If I told him of the three years spent trying, in a manner more patient than my first attempt, to get near enough to Hitler to kill him, he would no more have believed me than my interrogator in Stockholm had.

'And where do you want to go?'

'To join the armed forces of my country. And if I cannot, I will fight alone.'

Casimir's flame of outraged patriotism was easy to understand, but this man's country was in his spirit rather than in any land. He had been marked down for execution soon after the *Anschluss* when Hitler united Germany and Austria, and had taken refuge in Poland, where after the defeat he had begun to organize his own force in the little towns and villages of the Carpathians.

'Some of us have escaped from death or prison, some from the disgrace of serving Hitler,' he told me. 'Freedom or death! What a cliché! Every man is a slave and all he can expect from his master is generosity.'

He pointed to the two bodies lying apart under a tree of their own. 'It's sad to think of those two honest men, fathers of families perhaps, who served their country. Gladly? Resignedly? We shall never know. But the fault is theirs. They voted that clown into power. Don't you think it would be right to describe my command as the Educational Corps?'

'Yes, Herr Professor, though I don't agree that the fault is theirs.'

'Then you are sorry for them?'

'Not in the least. I once killed a man-eater. Being old and hungry, it was not his fault. But he had to die.'

'I think you are in love with death.'

'I have had for so long nothing else to be in love with.'

'Not life?'

'For a little while life gave me all I could ever ask. Now only death remains.'

'You talk like a Russian refugee,' he said cheerfully. 'This is the Tatra, not Montmartre. Have another drink!'

Peacefully we ate and drank in the moonlight, each suppressing his curiosity about the other. Moshe had found two German-speakers and was inspecting horses with a glass in his hand, taken back into memories beyond the reach of pain.

'From the little you have told me, I suspect your maternal grandfather must have been the Graf von Darmshof, but I am ignorant of his English descendants. It is better so. We should not try to find out names. No one can ever be sure that he will keep silence under all they can do to him. In these mountains I am known only as the Voevod.

'Darmshof's son and my father were pages at the imperial court together with a younger son of Prince Euersperg. They were nicknamed the Three Musketeers. Happy days in Vienna under Franz Josef and his half-wit ministers who landed Europe where it is! Euersperg married a Jewess. People still talk of their daughter. She had the fire and beauty of both the bloods. I saw her once. Irresistible! A man could create himself a poet just to pay tribute to her.'

Indeed he could. Dark, slender lioness of love and courage, who commands to this day my soul and inhibits my body from desire of any other woman. You, my treasure, whom I avenge.

'She gave those damn Austrian Nazis no peace,' he went on. 'Plotting violence for violence, it seems, as well as propaganda. She was often in England. You may have met her.'

Yes, first in Spain, where she had taken her mother for safety after Chancellor Dollfuss was assassinated on Hitler's order and it was believed that invasion of Austria would follow immediately. It did not, so she returned and she and her father reorganized the cells of international resistance.

'Names. You said we should not try to find them out,' I reminded him, 'but the leaders must know them – all of those names of honour and influence in army, the universities, the churches. Then in 1937, when the Nazis and their Austrian supporters burst in and raped the state, father and daughter were quietly removed to Germany.'

'Silence is the worst cruelty of dictatorship. There was a rumour that she was shot,' he said.

'Shot? Do you think they can be as merciful as that?'

I had not meant to say more, but he shared the memory of her, and from a single meeting.

'They split her apart slowly,' I told him, 'inch by inch between the questions, as if delivering a child that was too large. And still she would not talk. They let her die. She didn't count. After all she was only half Aryan.'

'How do you know?'

'Because her father told me. They made him watch. He gave the names they wanted but it was too late. He was sent home with a memory that was worse than torture. He killed himself.'

I could have taken his hand and sobbed like a child, but it was no more his business than that of the carrion lying under the trees.

3

Sentries were posted high above us. The camp of partisans slept on its hidden ledge. In the morning the Voevod asked me how I intended to reach the British army in the Middle East. I could only reply that I had always been a few hours ahead of capture and that until I fell in with Casimir I could not begin to make plans. My best hope was to reach Romania and then by sea, if it could be done, by sea to neutral Turkey.

'Have you any papers at all beyond those of Haase?' he asked.

'A valid passport in the name of Ernesto Menendez Peraza, landowner of Nicaragua.'

'But that would let you through.'

'It would – if Don Ernesto had not been involved in an attempt to assassinate Hitler.'

'Impossible unless one belonged to his entourage.'

'I was well on the way to that.'

'Would German frontier guards have your name on their blacklist?'

'Yes. At the top of it. But ordinary Romanian guards might not.'

'Well, I can help you on your way a little. We are running short of ammunition and I have learned that we may get it across the frontier in what was Russia. They left Poland in a hurry.'

The following night we set out, passing round the Dukla Peak and then south. The moon helped, but I was astonished how this pack of frontier wolves fat with flesh of the dead could keep on course across the featureless watershed, always ready if threatened to split up, radiating into the valley forests and reuniting after days of concealment. Every man was self-supporting in food and weapons.

Dawn after our second night's bivouac brought back memories of early youth. I knew where I was. Through a V between the hills I could catch a glimpse of the plain of the Tisza and see part of a broken line of wire and blockhouses which marked the frontier – a frontier which had only lasted two years.

The day was spent gathering more local intelligence. Our own Slovaks were out on foot mixing with the peasants. Two shepherds found us and gave us local news. We heard that nobody paid much attention to the former frontier, that it was very lightly garrisoned, and that it would take time to concentrate enough troops to hold us up on our passage from forest to forest. Not surprisingly I remember the tactical position very clearly. Though no soldier, I drew from it the lesson that it is intelligence which counts. Our daring Viennese commander made the mistake of Franz Josef and the Czechs in believing that no Slovaks were pro-German.

He decided to move down to agricultural land and take position in the evening just inside the last of the woods. There we had open country in front of us for four or five miles. We were to rush this in a bunch instead of sneaking over one by one or in small parties, and should reach safe refuge in the tangled foothills on the other side as the night closed in. Since our objective was to collect arms and ammunition from some small depot which the advancing Germans had not found or not bothered to find, it looked to me as if his retreat to his usual hunting grounds would be long and dangerous.

And so began my second battle. We emerged from the

trees in two ragged columns. To our right was open country with a couple of abandoned blockhouses; to our left, at
an angle of forty-five degrees to our advance, was a narrow
valley running up into the hills with a stream at the bottom.
The map showed another small stream running across our
front, not deep enough to form an obstacle.

We were all trotting fast to cross the long stretch of open
land and have time to find some easily defensible position for
the night. I was riding along near the front of the left-hand
column, remembering days of the 1920s and the adventurous
happy youth who cantered out into these valleys past peasants doffing their caps, when a blast of machine-gun fire hit
us from the front. My horse was shot under me in the best
tradition of wars of the last century and I pitched over its
shoulder in a fall more sudden than that of the hunting field
but no worse. Lying still with bullets spitting earth at me, I
vaguely recalled that cavalry horses some time somewhere
were trained to lie down while the rider fired over the body
as if it were a sandbag. That seemed hard on the horse, but
mine was already dead.

I slid into that useful cover and took a quick glance over
it. Half the left-hand column were down and the survivors
had raced for the nearby valley, the leaders galloping for the
shelter of the ravine bent low in the saddle. The right-hand
column had not suffered so badly and were off their horses
and returning the fire.

I unslung the Mannlicher and prepared to join in. It was
obvious what had happened. The enemy had learned of our
movements late in the day, and while we were still in the trees
short of the frontier had correctly assessed our intentions
and seized the opportunity for a successful ambush, moving
whatever men were available into the stream bed which ran
across our front. Casimir, whose secret campaign depended

on the apparent innocence and humility of his village cells and his own deadly skill as a double agent, would never have taken such a blind risk as our partisans.

Little could be seen of the enemy, but as they were not dug in they had to show occasional heads above the banks of the stream. The Mannlicher, now that we were on good terms, bagged a brace at two hundred yards. I had the impression that, fully engaged with our right column, they did not at first appreciate where the shots were coming from and opened up on the edge of the wood. That gave our right a moment of respite in which they attempted short rushes to get round the flank. Hopeless. Another machine-gun was on a fixed line of fire parallel to the enemy front.

Uniforms glimpsed – but too quickly for action – suggested that these frontier troops were Slovaks under experienced German command. They were showing no exaggerated enthusiasm for action. They ought to have been able to wipe us out instead of pinning us down. The detachment commander – an oldish man probably only fit for garrison duty in comparatively peaceful Slovakia – exposed himself with first-war resolution once too often to the Mannlicher. Slackening fire thereafter showed that morale was crumbling. But neither side were going to rise from the earth and risk annihilation before nightfall. Meanwhile I had proved to my own satisfaction that the rifle, given some cover and in the absence of mortar, was the superior arm. However, this last shot revealed my position. It was convenient to change horses – on the ground, that is.

In the deep dusk there was some movement. I could vaguely make out the Slovaks crawling like crocodiles out of the stream bed. There was some firing but, I think, no casualties. Then what was left of our right column rushed forward and found the position unoccupied. They caught the few horses which had bolted out of the line of fire and went straight on towards the distant wooded hills which had been our original objective. I did not follow. It occurred to me that the enemy might have fallen back to a more serious line where they could receive reinforcements and stop our escape.

The deep and narrow valley into which half of our left-hand column had galloped seemed a safe spot, so long as the head of it was not closed. So half a dozen of us disappeared into it carrying our wounded who had a chance of recovery. We were too small a band to have medical services or more than one primitive ambulance. A heartbreak. When we had gone we heard a few shots from men who had decided on death at their own hands rather than the enemy's. They knew there would be no mercy for them in the morning unless for those who were kept alive long enough to be interrogated. I believe there were no wounded left alive in the stream bed either. I decided that in future I would fight with regular troops or alone, but never again with guerillas.

As we advanced up the valley, the rising moon showed enough of it for me to recognize. There I had ridden as a boy. I had even killed a harmless wolf. My misgivings about the head of the valley increased. It became a gorge with few trees but steepish sides of limestone cracked, creviced and pinnacled. Plenty of cover there was, but both ends were remarkably easy to block.

We caught up the rest of the left column. They had suffered more severely than the right, and I was very glad to find Moshe unhurt. He appeared to prefer being shot at to shooting and was coolly patching up a neat hole in his horse's ear. The Voevod, in the way of commanders, was more inclined to congratulate the enemy than to blame himself. I told him all I knew of the lie of the land and advised him to reach the pines of the high forest before dawn if we had the strength, for there could be no doubt that we had stirred up a wasps' nest. He agreed that there might be trouble, but assured me that many times the enemy had triumphantly surrounded them and then found that there was nothing at all in the middle. He cursed those honest shepherds who had given him false information. He should have known, he said, that any of them who were left free to feed their flocks over those miles of abandoned fortifications must be on good terms with the patrols, German and Slovak. They did not seek vengeance as we did for innumerable brutalities but wanted only peace and a good price for spring lambs.

We were not out of the valley at dawn. We lost time crossing and recrossing the stream and twice hauled horses up promising slopes which ended in sheer ledges. Moon shadows, stretches of complete blackness, fantastic rock formations – whatever that crumbling, waterworn limestone could do, it did. Years ago it had made some sense to me, but then, in sunlight, one could see at a distance where there was a possible path and where there was not.

Daylight did show us that we were nearly there and that the valley ended in a slope of scree which could easily be traversed. We halted to draw breath and a moment later were diving for the cover of rocks, leaving two more of our dead on the ground. Further progress was impossible, and if our retreat too was blocked this was the end.

The way up and out of the valley had only been vaguely in my mind, for of course it offered no special difficulty to a boy who could leave his pony at the bottom and scramble up the scree if he wished. What I did remember, rather to the exclusion of all else, was a raven's nest to which I had climbed. It had been on the flat lip of a buttress thrust out from the cliff very near the top. A tangle of wind-swept sticks hanging over the edge showed that the nest was still there. It occurred to me that if I could get up our light machine-gun I should be well above the enemy position and in excellent cover.

'But are you sure you can get there?' the Voevod asked when I suggested my plan. He didn't want to lose his remaining gun before he had to when attacked from front and rear.

'Yes, with the help of two men. And one of them must know how to use it because I don't.'

'You astonish me!'

'Simple. I have been a hunter but never a soldier.'

'How long will it take you to get up there?'

'Twenty minutes at a guess.'

'Well, we can only hope we have that long.'

Our climb was out of sight of the enemy all the way, up a gully and then up the back of the crag which was pitted and jagged and safe enough if one avoided rotten stone. I went up first, found the nest disused and cleared away some of it which was occupying too much of the top. The remainder, an untidy mass of sticks and dead roots, speckled with white droppings, was perfect cover. I looked through it and was startled at what I saw. I saw above the machine-gun posts on both sides of the scree and above the even heathland behind it, where the enemy's front line was lying down in dead ground. The rest of the small but powerful force was idling and smoking a little way back, satisfied spectators of the destruction of this pestilent scourge of the Tatra frontiers. I was equally satisfied. They were all Germans. The ravens would not be hungry.

With aid of knotted reins, we pulled and pushed our machine-gun up and set it level. When he looked down, my able assistant could not believe his eyes any more than I. His first burst of plunging fire took out the gunners on both sides of the scree. The men lying on the edge jumped up and bolted back to the shelter of the scrubby woodland behind. Not many of them reached it, but those who did were not going to give in so lightly. They had spotted the raven's nest and shots splintered the crag below us or whined overhead. They then tried a move which I had never thought of, but was probably obvious to any professional. They broke out of the scrub and came bobbing along the top of the escarpment in order to get above us. We caused them some trouble but not enough since the angle of fire was difficult. It seemed to be an occasion for Lady Mannlicher, so I crawled to the back of the buttress and up the broken line of cliff behind it. There were six of these intruders, bold and clever but hopelessly exposed. Only two of them managed to crawl away. I was thankful the move had failed, for I was at last and finally out of ammunition.

We were clear of the trap which we had scurried into and at once struck north to the green forests and dark pines which were the natural home of the band. No time, thank God, could be wasted in stripping the wounded and shooting prisoners. We had to be far away when the force advancing along the rugged bottom of the valley climbed up to the scene where the ravens were already wheeling overhead. Our retreat could be tracked easily enough, but neither troop-carriers nor armour could ever get at us. I suspect that a follow-up by well-armed alpine infantry could have destroyed or dispersed us, but from the enemy point of view was such an operation worth the butcher's bill?

After nightfall we were safe and the survivors of our right-hand column were drifting in. They were all infinitely grateful to me and presented me with a decoration: the bottom of a can of tomatoes within a circle of oak leaves. There were roars of laughter – the relief from thirty hours of tension

– when I replied that I accepted it not for valour but for an excellent memory.

They pressed me to stay with them, but understood that I wanted to reach the army of the Middle East. Although I thought it very unlikely that I should ever again have such an opportunity for personal vengeance, I knew – which I did not tell them – that I should soon find the barbarities of guerilla warfare unendurable. When I was alone with the Voevod, I did touch distantly on the question. He replied at once, 'No need for such tact, friend. What do you suggest I do with prisoners?'

There was no possible answer. One could, I suppose, drag them around from mountain to mountain at a horse's tail, or exchange them under a flag of truce, but the SD would have ensured that there was no one alive to exchange them for.

'I would have taken you nearer to Romania, if we hadn't been caught in those damned fields,' he said, 'but now we shall have to fall back into Poland and re-form. If you and your good Jew wish to go on alone, I can let you have a Romanian from the Bucovina who has business across the frontier and can be your guide. He speaks German; his name is Vasile Cantescu.'

I asked if he were trustworthy, for I thought it likely he would be anti-Russian rather than anti-German.

'Trustworthy, yes. I know he was condemned to death.'

'And he dares to go back?'

'He will cross the frontier as a poor farmer from the Bucovina who was stripped by the Russians of everything he possessed. Such refugees are welcome if their birth certificates show they are pure Romanian. He won't stay long – just to see a friend, he says.'

'How far is it to the frontier?'

'About seventy miles. Say, four days. I can spare you food, and is there anything else I can do for you?'

I told him there were two things. One was any old horse for Moshe; the other was to return the Mannlicher to Casimir whenever he had a chance, telling him that it had served well till the last round. That he promised to do.

'And never forget that Romania is Hitler's loyal ally,' he added, 'stuffed with troops and SD. If you surface at all, you'll be interned or worse. So what will you do for money?'

'I have enough German marks for a few days. As an outlaw I've needed no money. A rare advantage. Perhaps I can reach the Danube.'

'Not unless you have local help. Somewhere there exists an underground, but I suspect it will be more use to Shapir than to you.'

There is little to tell of our journey. It was the same old story: up and down from forest to forest, plodding along over grass and moorland and always trying to keep some breast of the hills between ourselves and other travellers. Moshe and I were indistinguishable from peasants, filthy, bearded, wrapped in rags and sheepskins. Only Haase's excellent boots remained, under their coating of mud, fit for human society. Cantescu was rather more respectable. In an emergency he was to ride the horse and we should follow behind, thus giving a picture of a poor farmer and two of his men.

Once, we nearly ran into the Hungarian frontier by mistake and hastily retreated – at least I thought it was by mistake, till Cantescu cheerfully admitted that he wanted to find out exactly where he was.

In time of peace and mutual jealousies such a journey would have been most difficult but, as it was, Germans and Russians were slogging it out on the other side of the Black Sea and token forces from Hitler's New European Order were with them. Except in Poland, frontiers were largely nominal and garrisons reduced.

We aimed to enter Romania at Sighet, leaving behind the vast German-occupied mess. On the night before we came down from the watershed we went into committee to decide on a plan if controls were hostile and too inquisitive. Cantescu was all right. He had his birth certificate showing him to be a Romanian citizen from the Bucovina. That would give him entry. It looked as if Moshe Shapir, recognizable as a Jew and with no papers at all, would have to cross the frontier illegally. As I was much more likely to succeed in that than he, I was prepared to lend him the passport of Don Ernesto, who was making his way from Poland to the sea in the hope of getting home.

'What a pity you speak only German!' I exclaimed.

'And of course my native language.'

'What's that?'

'Spanish.'

I should have guessed it. Those keen, aristocratic features were of course those of a Sephardic Jew.

I examined him closely as if I myself were a customs officer. Cleaned up, with his owl's nest of a beard neatly trimmed and preserving Don Ernesto's moustache, he could perfectly well be a descendant of the Spanish conquerors. But still there were difficulties in fitting his description to the passport which had served both me and von Lauen. He was not tall enough. His eyes were brown, not grey. His hair was dark, not fair.

Cantescu said cheerfully that we should leave it to him. He admitted that he was always inclined to blind ahead. A Romanian, he said, should not bother planning for trouble but talk his way out of it when it came. He thought I ought to stick to Don Ernesto's passport and that Moshe should be my faithful servant who had had money and passport stolen. He was sure he could fix it. We must remember that Romanians were a Latin people, isolated at the back end of Europe and specially obliging to other Latins. All we needed was a pair of scissors and a good wash. Failing scissors, he would sharpen his hunting knife and do his best.

Hairdressing with a knife is a process I could recommend to the Gestapo, especially when one has only the flames of a fire to give light. Stretching fingerful after fingerful, he took off my beard, leaving me with the wreck of a moustache and a bleeding lip. He then started on Moshe, giving him a pointed Velasquez beard and a rather better moustache than mine. We came out horridly unshaven, as was natural enough for travellers, but obviously gentlemen down on their luck. We had to promote the distinguished Moshe from servant to secretary.

In the early morning we went down into the foothills and on towards the fast and shining river beyond which was Romania. I was in no mood to welcome it, nervously assuring myself of the long odds against Romanian security officers being warned that Don Ernesto Menendez Peraza, killed in the bombing attack of Rostock, was very much alive, and that there was still nothing to connect Don Ernesto with the SD officer at Stettin, Auschwitz and Cracow. All the same, I nearly turned back when I spotted a couple of black German uniforms among the greys and blues of the Romanian army and officials.

At the barrier we presented ourselves, our horse and our papers. Moshe and I had agreed that he spoke only Spanish and I Spanish and German; so we stood by looking bewildered and as dignified as our dirty sheepskins permitted while Cantescu told our story. On his way back to his dear homeland he had come across us on foot in the Tatra, our car waylaid and stolen by Slovakian bandits when we were driving down to Romania. As we were obviously persons of some importance, he had taken pity on us and guided us to the frontier.

It was then my turn. Since the visas on my passport showed that I had resided in Berlin and had legally entered Denmark and Sweden I could not invent a better story than the truth. I said that I had hoped to get home to Nicaragua from Sweden but could not. My secretary and I therefore decided to try and reach neutral Turkey and see what chance we had there.

The officer returned my passport after taking longish notes and told me that he would have to refer the matter to other authorities – which, I feared, meant those hangers-on of the Gestapo. He would not accept poor Moshe at all.

Cantescu protested, but the conversation was courteous and appeared to be leading somewhere.

'He wants to know where you got the horse,' he said. 'I told him you had bought it from a gypsy.'

There was more cordial conversation.

'He says that horses are scarce in this part of the country. The Germans collected all they could and the Russians took the lot from the Bucovina when they retreated. He would allow me to take it in if it belonged to me.'

'It can belong to the devil for all I care.'

'Patience! Would you like to give it to me as a reward for saving your lives? And it had better be in writing.'

I scribbled a sort of deed of gift, and Cantescu and I shook hands on it while the immigration officer beamed at us.

'I am now going through with the horse and you will not see any more of me till perhaps this evening. For the present, you and Moshe will have to wait, but when you are allowed into Sighet you will find that I have booked you a room at the hotel.'

I still did not understand. I said goodbye to Cantescu warmly but suspected he was talking us into trouble, not out of it. Then Moshe and I sat down on a melancholy bench in the waiting room, where at least we were brought a slab of sausage and a carafe of plum brandy. We were there till mid-afternoon, when the officer returned, saluted me, put an arm across Moshe's shoulders and told us we were free to leave. A grubby one-horse cab awaited us and took us to the small hotel, white and with little welcoming windows. The Middle East was that much nearer but there was still a nagging fear in my mind of those apparently idle black uniforms and the notes that the grey uniform had taken.

A barber's shop was still open. Afterwards we sat down to an excellent meal, Moshe resembling the Velasquez at which Cantescu's hunting knife had aimed, I once more Don Ernesto. Rather to my surprise, Cantescu turned up to help us with our bottle. I congratulated him on his country's officials, who seemed most reasonable.

'His brother has a farm,' he explained, 'but not a horse in sight and he is nearly ruined. When I heard that, I felt so sorry for him that I offered him ours. And, as soon as I had quietly stabled the horse where he instructed me, he kept his word and let you pass. A reasonable arrangement between two honest men.'

He told me that I could safely stay in the hotel for the night, having been cleared by frontier controls. Next day I must move. He would tell me where. My passport should be good enough for hotels and railways.

'In a few minutes Shapir and I will go for a stroll in the dusk. Don't say goodbye and look as if you were expecting him back. One never knows what eyes are watching.'

I had told Moshe that I would never leave him until he was in safety or dead. We had not mentioned the promise since, but I knew well that it had kept him going when he should have collapsed. So I said to Cantescu that I would only hand him over to his own people.

'Good – if he can find any.'

'It's as bad as that?'

'Worse.'

'But all I know is what the Voevod told me: that you are not and never were a farmer from the Bucovina and that you were condemned to death.'

'That is all you need to know. But if I was to be shot I must have escaped and I must have had helpers. Never mind who they were. I have reason to believe they might set Shapir on his road to Palestine, though God knows if he'll get there. Fake Nicaraguan passports call for different treatment.'

'This man is a Jew in heart,' Moshe gallantly declared.

'He may be in heart but not in other places. Don't worry about him, dear Shapir. There are many of us who admire the British, and not all roads lead to Jerusalem.'

'But I must know which road he will take.'

'And he would like to know what road you will take. I will only tell you both what you already know: that death is close behind you. Trust me to make him keep his distance.'

We had been together long enough for me to recognize a man of tenacity and finesse, though the days were only an interval between his unknown future. So far as I was concerned, I was ready to trust him, but Moshe must decide for himself. I felt that if he left with Cantescu it would be because he considered he was a hindrance to me, and I reminded him that twice he had probably saved my life – once by common sense, and once by sheer courage.

He answered me by getting up to go with Cantescu, and our eyes had to speak for us since we were allowed no show of emotion and no goodbyes.

In the morning I paid my bill and found that my store of marks would still be enough for second-class travel, food and bed for a couple of nights. I explained with a smutty wink that my secretary, after long privation, had found other accommodation for the night. That done, I waited in the bar for something to happen. If nothing happened, the innocent landowner from Nicaragua would take a train to Bucharest or the mouth of the Danube. Meanwhile I just waited like any commercial traveller stranded in the third-rate hotel of some provincial town. I regretted the forests of the Tatra and the comforting Mannlicher slung on my back.

Life began again when the hotel porter handed me an envelope addressed to Don Ernesto. It contained nothing but a third-class ticket to Bucharest by the evening train. At the station I found my way on to the train with a crowd of peasants and settled down on a slatted wooden seat, of which I occupied eighteen inches between some underpaid clerk who reeked of pickled cucumber and a variety of coarse perfumes from – at a guess – the local whore house, and on the other side a hearty, drunken yeoman of the Bucovina who continually farted, laughed and apologized. It occurred to me, however, that my clothes were possibly an equal offence to the company, though my body was well washed, and that the donor of my ticket had been right to choose the third class.

We travelled all night with both my neighbours dozing on my shoulders. Intimacy without speech. Romanian I recognized as a Latin language, but it was incomprehensible. At eleven in the morning we piled out on to Bucharest station. My papers were inspected and my ticket collected, and I set out into a busy city of low white houses and trees and tram-lines and poverty, already in the pleasant heat of early summer. I presumed that since I had been given a ticket someone must be observing my movements, and when I came to a café sat down at an outside table where I could easily be seen and discreetly contacted if the someone chose to come closer.

Before long a taxi drew up alongside the café and the driver reported to me exactly as if I had ordered it. I got in and we drove across a handsome boulevard and away to a suburb of small houses and yards which looked unchanged since Bucharest was a large village. Here were no arrogant German military to be seen, though in the main streets they had been scattered about like spots on a sufferer from measles. The car stopped in a small square with an onion-domed church in the centre, and the driver signalled to me to get out. As I made as if to pay him, he gave me in French some such directions as: first right, second left, No. 11, go straight in.

I went straight in and found myself in a simple room with a bed made up and a dressing gown lying on it, a comfortable chair, a table set with coffee, rolls and a carafe of plum brandy and, best of all, a civilized lavatory and shower. So I was expected and my probable needs foreseen. White-washed walls were decorated with Romanian rugs, giving a somewhat oriental effect. I might have been in some one-room annexe to the house of a Christian Arab.

I threw into a corner my sheepskin and the now ragged suit which Casimir had given me, took a shower, put on the dressing gown and breakfasted. It all seemed the lap of luxury to Don Ernesto. Death, as Cantescu had warned, might be looking over my shoulder, but meanwhile I revelled in the touch of a silk dressing gown which called for Noël Coward to do it justice.

Thinking that it was about time I had some instructions, I waited for my host. Assuming that the people who had marked me down in spite of the crowded station knew what they were doing, I left the door unlocked as I had found it.

Anybody could walk in and I might have to explain who I was and what was my business, when I had no idea what I should say and what I shouldn't.

There were curious faint thumps from the lavatory which I put down to whims of Romanian plumbing. The door was opened from the inside by a woman who remarked in charmingly accented English, 'Good morning, Don Ernesto.'

'Good morning, madam. May I thank you and congratulate you on your efficiency?'

'If spiders can come up, I can.'

'Then at last I have found someone who can tell me why they aren't drowned. What I meant was that I don't see how your people spotted me on the station.'

'Oh, that was easy. Cantescu had a man travelling on the train.'

She was in her early thirties and lovely as well as witty: dark hair, laughing grey eyes, classical features which were not too severe, and skin, to judge by her forearms in a summer frock, as soft as the bloom on a fruit. At first I thought her slightly tanned by sun, but later I found that Romanian women gave an impression of pink and white over tan rather than the other way round.

'A lot of trouble for a Slovakian bandit.'

'But for a British agent no trouble is enough.'

I foresaw unnecessary complications if I passed myself off as an accredited spy and was then put in touch with secret operators, who would inevitably suspect that I was in enemy pay and clumsily trying to infiltrate their organization.

'I am British but not an agent.'

'That was what the Voevod thought. He called you a fighting man, too proud for a spy.'

'It's true I don't like the Nazis.'

'Don't like! You are a flame of hatred, he said.'

'How do you know all this?'

'I travel sometimes, but in first class. And it seems there is another side to you. You remember Mr Shapir?'

'I only parted from him the day before yesterday.'

'He said to the Voevod that never in his life had he known such love and tenderness.'

It was an extraordinary tribute from Moshe, to whom, I should have thought, I gave the impression of a ruthless killer.

'He is safe?'

'What a question! Are you? Am I? I don't know where he is. Sometimes Cantescu exchanges information with quite a different underground. Tomorrow or the next day your Moshe will be under their wing. But you must stay here until we have a sure route to Turkey for you. Show me what papers you have!'

I gave her the Nicaraguan passport, telling her that it belonged to one of Hitler's agents, whom I had killed. The trouble was that the SD knew it and were on the lookout for me all over occupied Europe.

'And you have nothing else?'

I slit open the wide hem of my sheepskin coat and produced Haase's documents.

'To start with I had his uniform too, and it helped me to escape from Germany. But no one could mistake the photograph for me.'

'This Haase reported direct to the heads of the SD,' she exclaimed. 'We must fix the photograph. I am sure we can.'

'If your forger is reliable. Otherwise a word from him and it's the end of us.'

'You will not mind if I come to talk to you from time to time? The spider will be careful not to come up when you are – well, engaged.'

'And may I know how she gets in?'

'The floor of your shower cabinet is hinged and steps lead up from a passage. It's not dug out. It's the cellar of a house which was knocked down in the earthquake and my friends and I built this room on top. We foresaw trouble before the Germans arrived. I sometimes entertain the least awful of the officers. Very correct they are. They like to think I am a true Aryan princess.'

'I am not surprised.'

'Straight out of Wagner? For God's sake, no! I am descended from Byzantine emperors. Lovely pure blood! Greeks, barbarians, Egyptians and probably the odd eunuch. There were three kinds of them, you know, and the imperial gelders didn't always make a proper job of it.'

A complex creature, that mermaid-spider! Evidently it was assumed by the enemy that such an aristocrat must be anti-Russian. Well, of course she was, and that made her contempt for Hitler and his Nazis easier to disguise.

'What am I to call you?'

'Just Domnitza – the little lady.'

She sat on the bed flicking one crossed leg as if the pointed toe were a dagger. By way of the Voevod and his exploits, she led me back into the last century, rightly or wrongly envied. People forget that the Austro-Hungarian was not the only empire in Europe, she said. In the Ottoman empire injustices and corruption were obscene but it ruled its subjects according to established laws, without regard to religion, language or blood.

'The Voevod's ancestors and mine were governors of great provinces,' she went on. 'I expect they were thoroughly disliked by their subjects but they made no distinctions between them. So we loathe the Nazis and their cruel myths only fit for little bourgeois without any reason for pride.'

An interesting theory. But I think she and the Voevod

had made it up to account for a hatred which was only due to outraged humanity.

'Now we must get you some decent clothes,' she said, 'so that you can move on the streets when the time comes. I have brought a tape measure. What class would you like to belong to?'

'Poor, but honest. Some craftsman who can only afford one suit every three years, and the cloth must last.'

The intimacy of measurement was pleasurable but no more than a sister's caress. When a man has loved as I, he remembers too clearly the divine dual surrender of the spirits for any imitation by mere bodies to be tolerable.

I felt secure in that room of hers. A new sensation. I had not felt secure since that summer of 1938 when I had Hitler in my sights. Meals came up through the shower cabinet carried by a manservant who tidied the place and spoke only Romanian, When I asked Domnitza how she managed to keep my presence secret to the kitchen staff, she told me that she had a small stove in her private apartment on the ground floor and that she had accustomed servants to a pretended habit of preparing favourite dishes herself. Only the manservant and her personal maid knew of the existence of the secluded room, and they were none too sure whether occupants were lovers or political dissidents.

'It held Cantescu for a few days before we got him away,' she said.

'I hear he was condemned to death.'

'Oh, nothing so legal as that. We grabbed him with only minutes to spare. He tried to poison the dictator Antonescu, and the wrong man drank the cup. Medieval, isn't it? All was faultlessly planned but he didn't bother to protect himself from suspicion. He didn't care what happened to him, but we did. Antonescu is a personal friend of Hitler, which meant that every torturer in the Reich would be encouraged to try his skill on Cantescu.'

'They didn't search your house?'

'They searched the house of everyone who knew him but found nothing. Such a lot of apologies I had.'

My feeling of security was somewhat dented after that, though she had intended to give me added confidence. Cool and daring were these resisters of rank, but I could not help thinking they took unnecessary risks: the Voevod with the stream across his front; Cantescu at the frontier; Domnitza, who had just told me more than I ought to know; the taxi driver. However, their organization was none of my business.

My suit, when it appeared, was of brown serge, hideous, indestructible as old friendship but infernally hot in the flowering June of Bucharest. I'd have been glad of it in the high Carpathians, and under a bit of waving green stuff it would make good camouflage. The photograph on Haase's comprehensive pass was a perfect job. Domnitza herself had taken it, laughing at her attempts to get me to compose my face into the stolid insensitivity of a Gestapo officer. Her tame craftsman – there was another fellow who held our lives in his hands – had successfully reproduced the embossed stamp, but, if anyone had reason to suspect it and used a magnifying glass, he could detect that one photograph had been substituted for another.

When all was ready, Domnitza advised me to spend a day in the outside world to give myself confidence. I now had three different proofs of identity. Hidden in the lining of the brown serge suit were Haase's papers, and Don Ernesto's passport. In my pocket was the identity card of a Greek seaman from a coaster plying between Romanian and Turkish ports. My Greek was not nearly good enough but would pass so long as I was not speaking to a Greek.

The day of normal city life did indeed give me confidence. I lunched. I spoke in deliberately bad French and German. I sat in public parks. I was only an ant in an anthill. When again I entered my private apartment I found Domnitza sitting on my bed wearing the Noël Coward dressing gown and only enough else to be provocative. I was infinitely sad. I felt as I might if coldly returning a bunch of wild flowers to some child who had picked them for me.

'You said there were three kinds of eunuch at the emperor's palace, Domnitza. Here is a fourth.'

'Who is she?' she asked.

At the time I took her response as extraordinary insight, but perhaps it was not all that extraordinary. She knew how irresistible she was; she knew from my eyes, after nearly a week of intimacy, that I admired both her beauty and intelligence, and she realized, I suppose from my bearing and my past, that I was a whole man, so she arrived at the correct explanation.

'I am faithful to the dead.'

'Or to death itself?'

The Voevod had said that, but as a statement not a question.

'I am in love with killing those who killed her.'

'Can't you forget, my dear?'

'No more than I could forget you, if it had been you.'

'Only a sweet speech to stay with me after you have gone?'

That night I was woken up by the familiar swish of the shower cabinet. I hoped Domnitza was not returning to cause us both more embarrassment; on the other hand, I could never be anything but glad to listen to her voice and luxuriate in her beauty as I would – though the parallel is far from exact – in full moonlight on a calm sea or among the breasts and hanging woods of my beloved English downland.

A complete stranger entered my room, an old man with a bushy white beard who would have looked like Father Christmas except that he was very formally dressed with a white slip under his waistcoat. He was obviously a prince or politician of the old school up from his remote estate in the country. I wondered if he could possibly be Domnitza's grandfather.

'Cantescu, and at your service,' he said with a slight and graceful bow.

The disguise was perfect down to the lines on face and forehead. I doubt if he could have walked the streets by day as so distinguished a character. Passers-by would have saluted him feeling that they ought to know who he was though they didn't. But at night one would have the good manners not to look too closely at this personage, already in the history books, on his discreet and dignified way to his mistress.

'And where have you left your carriage and pair?' I asked.

'In the square,' he replied.

I could not tell whether that was the incredible truth or whether he was just answering jest with jest. He went on to say that the more conspicuous you made yourself, the less likely you were to be a wanted man – typical of these daring and debonair Romanians, but I doubt it.

He had dropped in on me to arrange what he called a few details of my departure.

'Tomorrow we are proposing to ship you on an oil tanker from the port of Constanza to Istanbul. You are a Greek seaman off a barge laid up in the Danube and you want to go home. The papers are very simple and we can manage them, all properly stamped. I don't know what action the Turks will take – probably put you on any Greek caïque in the harbour. But you'll have every chance to run for the British consulate.'

It looked as if it might be the same old game. No proof of British nationality. Where have you been? How long? Why?

But once ashore in Turkey I could somehow reach the army. From Sweden I could not.

I felt that Cantescu was a little too fascinated by disguises, secret refuges and the easy corruption of minor servants of state. He and Domnitza had been quite right to keep me away from hotels and any other activities which involved registration with the police and their Gestapo associates; but since I had passed the Sighet controls and was legally in Romania it seemed to me that I could be safely shipped to Istanbul as Don Ernesto. True, I had no visa to enter Turkey. However, if he could have me smuggled ashore as a Greek seaman, he ought to be able to do it equally well as the Nicaraguan landowner.

Too much of a risk, he said. A boatman could cheaply and easily be persuaded to row a seaman to a dark beach or watersteps and take him back again, but not a suspiciously respectable passenger. Also, I must not forget those two black-uniformed watchers at Sighet who might by now have examined the Romanian records and could be on my trail.

To that I objected that it would take time for officials at the port of Constanza to send in their returns to headquarters and by then the tanker would be at sea.

'They are not as inefficient as all that,' Cantescu said. 'Most of the traffic in the Black Sea is military, so they have plenty of time to check passengers.'

I still would not give way. I did not like his casual phrase that I would have 'every chance to run for the British consulate'. I might have none. At least the Nicaraguan passport would prevent me from being returned to the ship. So we compromised. If I insisted on taking the risk I could go on board as Don Ernesto but I must land as a nameless seaman. The oil engineer acting as supercargo was a trustworthy, well-paid agent. I should recognize him by his slicked-down grey hair. During the twenty hours or so of the passage I should not contact him, but on arrival at Istanbul he would make the arrangements for smuggling me ashore and tell me what to do.

The plan once settled, I asked about Moshe Shapir. Had he been got away in a false beard and the robes of a Greek Orthodox bishop? But Cantescu was no more in a mood for light-heartedness. His responsibilities were too real and too urgent. He replied that he did not know how the underground run to Palestine was organized, but thought it probable that Moshe would be passed from hand to hand till he was in Turkey, and after that the Moslems, unlike so-called Christians, would have no special interest in hunting him down.

I left next day as secretly as I had arrived, carrying a small case containing toiletries and that invaluable sheepskin coat, now cleaned and de-loused, with Hauptmann Haase's papers in the lining. Domnitza did not come to say goodbye but sent me by the manservant a small locket, which opened into a diptych showing on one leaf an icon of St Jerome and on the other the head and shoulders of some Byzantine princess so like her that her meaning was clear.

In the square I found the same taxi which had collected me from the café and the same silent driver. The road to Constanza was badly worn and we passed convoy after convoy of troops, on their way, I suppose, from Bulgaria and Greece to the Russian front. This show of power did not depress me – apart from wishing that I was behind the sandhills with an anti-tank gun – for this was the final leg of my journey to neutral Turkey and on at last to my own people and a war which need no longer be private.

The taxi dropped me well away from the port offices and discreetly vanished. I had no difficulty in passing through the security controls and even received good wishes. My long voyage home to Nicaragua by way of Istanbul, Egypt and round the Cape struck them as unusually adventurous and frustrated by long delays. I was advised to stay in Turkey till the end of the war, which after the sweeping victories of the Reich could not be far off.

I was rowed out to the loaded tanker. No cabin had been prepared for me but I was allowed to doss down in the sick bay. We sailed in the evening, and the following day, late in the afternoon, were anchored off the oil terminal at Istanbul. Some of the officers went ashore on the ship's business, among them the grey-haired supercargo who I hoped was attending to my business as well. I waited for his return in the sick bay, where I could be contacted less publicly than on deck.

He called on me after dark. He spoke French, like most educated Romanians, and told me that all was arranged. At ten o'clock – or as near to it as any Turk was likely to get – there would be a boat close under the bows and a rope hanging down from the rail. The deck would be empty except for the anchor watch, and I should make sure that none of them was anywhere near when I slid down the rope. The boatman would take me into the press of ferryboats on the Stamboul waterfront, one of which had been told to row me across the Horn to Pera.

The plan worked with a precision which surprised me, though it was far from easy to descend the rope with a case in one hand, even one as light as mine. As we drifted silently away into the reflected lights of the city, I saw the supercargo hauling in the rope. We passed under the bridge and there, side by side on the Stamboul waterfront, were the little ferries. One of them drew alongside and I was transferred to it un-observed with again that remarkable precision. Unobserved, too, I was landed at dark steps on the other side of the Horn. The Romanian agent seemed most efficient. I had now only to walk to the consulate, and Cantescu had explained to me exactly where it was.

At the top of the steps my arms were seized by a man on each side of me and a gun shoved in my back. They ordered me to come with them without any fuss. Since they were speaking German and sure that I understood it, the game was up, but I pretended to think they were a pair of ordinary thugs, dropped my case and offered to show them that the contents were of no value. Ordered to pick it up and come along, I managed to slip Don Ernesto's deadly passport out of my pocket and, when I stood up, to push it over the edge of the steps with my foot. That efficiency which I had admired could now be explained. The supercargo was a double agent profitably working for both the Romanian underground and the SD's bureau in Turkey.

I was driven up the hill to Galata and led into a pleasant little mansion which had no pretensions to secrecy. No doubt the British operatives were equally well known to the Turks and made themselves just as comfortable. As was proper in a neutral country, nobody was in uniform and the room to which I was taken for interrogation might have been the office of any prosperous merchant. The man facing me across the desk was, however, true to the clean national type: a large, beer-sodden, greasy Aryan with pimples on his forehead.

'Who are you? A Pole? Romanian?'

I answered that he had no right to question me, that I would explain my movements to Turkish police and no one else.

'Search him!'

They went through my case right down to the toothpaste and shaving soap. Then they stretched out the faithful sheepskin coat and felt it over, at once discovering the packet of Hauptmann Haase's papers.

'Triumph, major! We have caught the missing Haase!'

I remained silent. It looked as if my painstaking arrangements for the death of Ernesto Menendez Peraza and disappearance of Haase in the bombing of Rostock had been successful. It was plain that Don Ernesto was assumed to be dead and his name had never reached any blacklist.

'Swine! Deserter! Murderer of your comrades! And now caught on your way to the enemy!'

My only hope was to show calm and confidence.

'I must ask you, major, to look carefully at my documents. You will see that I am entitled to report directly to the headquarters of the Sicherheitsdienst. I can only tell you that I have been on special duty connected with the infiltration of the Romanian underground which, you will appreciate, could be a danger to our lines of communication. I know nothing of any murders, and I require you to explain the folly of arresting me when it was essential that my presence in Istanbul should not be known.'

'Folly of arresting! You who have connived at the escape of prisoners, slaughtered guards and then gunned down the detachment sent to capture you!'

So it had been decided that the mysterious Gestapo officer who had committed all these crimes was Haase.

'And deserter too?' I asked ironically.

He started to pound the desk while beads of sweat appeared among the pimples. I had him shaken.

'Confess what happened after the raid on Rostock!'

'With pleasure. My orders were to interrogate a certain person in Rostock and to take action immediately upon any information received before his associates could be aware of his arrest. He was due to die anyway but was killed in the raid.'

'Can that be confirmed by Berlin?'

'Of course, if they choose to do so. And at the same time I shall be compelled to report that a most secret mission has been aborted by the officious idiocy of a bunch of petty policemen who should never have been allowed to enter the service.'

'With your permission, sir ...' began the only one of my kidnappers who was not impressed, 'it is possible that this fellow is not Haase but has Haase's papers.'

I remarked, still contemptuous, that the stamped photograph in that case could not possibly fit me.

I lost a trick there. The major, though obviously reluctant to accept the advice of a subordinate, picked up his telephone and demanded, 'Is there anyone here who has served with a Hauptmann Haase and knows him?'

There was a considerable delay while I stood motionless – the picture, I hoped, of a correct German officer whose honour had been unjustly attacked. The answer came back that no one knew a Haase, but that the Salonica office might.

'Send a signal at once requesting urgent reply!'

'You think it wise?' I asked.

'Owing to the strategic importance of Salonica, the office is heavily staffed. There is a good chance that somebody will know you.'

It was a hopeful sign that he said 'know you' not 'know Haase'. But if there was somebody in Salonica who did know Haase it was the end of me. The only comforting thought was that as a deserter impersonating Haase I should be cleanly shot, whereas Ernesto, the so-nearly-successful assassin of Hitler, was destined to be kept alive so long as there was enough left of him to answer yes or no.

While we waited, the major was almost cordial and asked me to sit down. The two thugs, however, remained behind my chair. After a long pause, I remarked casually as one officer to another, 'What I cannot understand is why I should have been posted as a deserter.'

'It looks to me, if I may say so, as if you should have reported before leaving.'

'To whom? They were all dead or had run off in a panic. Unlike you and me, most of them had never heard a shot fired before.'

That pleased him, especially since I am sure he had never heard a shot fired himself. In anger, that is. Executions don't count.

'There seems to have been a slip-up somewhere,' I went on. 'But I do suggest these fellows of yours should not have acted so precipitately on a report from some Romanian seaman, probably a double agent, that some scoundrel of a resistance fighter was to be secretly landed.'

The reply from Salonica came in. Yes, the head of the Gestapo knew Haase well and would be most willing to identify him. He had always considered it absurd that such a man could be accused of desertion and murder. The major might safely discuss the matter by telephone and it was unnecessary to mention names or military details. From the ensuing conversation I gathered that the Gestapo chief regretted that he was too busy to fly to Istanbul but saw no reason why the officer in question should not be flown to Salonica.

The major was inclined to snort and bumble – I suppose because I was being taken out of his jurisdiction and he might be done out of the credit of either catching me or releasing me. One of his aides made up his mind for him by saying that there was a plane going to Salonica in the morning.

'It's laid on for General Kurtbek of the Turkish Ordnance.

I'll find out if there is room for two civilians. But the Turks will need proof of identity. Suppose this man refuses to go and asks for help?'

'If he does, it's proof enough that he isn't Haase. We can then get the Turks to take him over as an illegal immigrant and later have him extradited on a charge of murder.'

It was time for me to show the indignation that the real Haase would have done.

'This is all pig swill,' I stormed. 'I am what my documents say I am. I am not likely to sing out at the airport. Order the consul to issue a passport for me in any name you please! It must all be done discreetly, and as soon as I am identified I must be returned at once to Istanbul to carry out my assignment.'

By now they had all accepted the probability that I really was Hauptmann Haase of the Sicherheitsdienst and that Haase was not that mysterious officer who had left behind such a trail of devastation at Stettin and on the road to Cracow. The major actually apologized to me for the accommodation he was compelled to offer for the night. It was their prison cell but he was sure I would understand that, though he did not doubt my word, he was bound officially to take precautions. They would make it as comfortable as they could. They did, throwing a mat over a patch of bloodstains, giving me sheets as well as blankets, and providing a chamber pot with the head of Churchill on the bottom. Typical humour. I used the washbasin.

Early in the morning a German passport in the name of Ludwig Weber was brought to me to sign. My case and Haase's documents were returned. We left for the airport. My guard – one of the kidnappers – was armed and made sure that I could see he was.

All night the possibilities of any escape at all had been

running through my head in the intervals of dozing. So much depended on actual conditions during the drive to the airport and on arrival that I refused to take any firm decision. But now that we were on our way I had to make an instant choice between two alternatives both likely to end in my execution. On these occasions one does not reason but thinks in pictures. I saw myself visited in a Turkish gaol by the British consul uncertain whether this Ludwig Weber was a German deserter or a British traitor. I wasn't going to play the escaped prisoner-of-war again. Then extradition – or, if that was too much trouble, found to have committed suicide in my cell, thanks to a bribable Turkish gaoler.

Nothing, nothing. Again no proof of nationality. Again to be humiliated as an enemy of my country. Those damned three years in Germany. To hell with their acceptance or rejection. Revenge was what I wanted. The memory of Domnitza had curiously revived still more memories of my love and revived anger too. A second picture came up of sun on the mountainsides and seas of Greece if ever I could reach them. Yes, rather than rot among the prisons and intrigues and secret agents of shadowed Istanbul, I would go to Salonica.

The plane was a little Fokker with four seats behind the pilot. To preserve the decencies, I was presented to General Kurtbek as a distinguished German industrialist. He sat on my left with the Gestapo guard behind us and turned out, like so many of the upper class of his country, to have the affability of a genial European and the courtesy of a Moslem gentleman. His uniform was more or less British with Sam Browne belt and revolver.

We soon got into conversation, using English, which he spoke with an entertaining blend of guttural accent and clipped British army speech. After relations had been established, he appreciated that he was not going to be bored during the hour and a half's flight to Salonica. He knew of course a great deal about the Russians and had a high opinion of their strategy which, he thought, Hitler underrated.

Ludwig Weber complained that before the war the Turkish army had been largely equipped by the British and added, 'You are not coming in on their side, I hope.'

'You bet your life we are not,' he replied.

I remember that exact idiomatic answer.

'I am going to Salonica to examine some of your latest armour. Your Mark IV tank is better than anything the British have got.'

An inspiration. I saw half a chance. And my guard did not speak English.

'Better soldiers than we expected,' I said, 'but poorly equipped. For example take that .38 you have there. It's badly balanced.'

He did exactly what I had dared to hope – pulled it out of the holster and weighed it on the palm of his right hand. I grabbed it, whipped round, shot my guard and finished him off with a second.

'Don't move, sir! I mean you no harm at all.'

I then dealt with the startled pilot.

'You will make a course for Thessaly. I warn you that I know Greece well. I also warn you that I shall be shot when we reach Salonica so I don't mind if I die now. Don't touch your radio! You will put us down somewhere flat in the valley of the Aliakmon.'

I turned to the general, who appeared less worried than I was, sitting back and enjoying the theatre.

'Do you know Macedonia, sir?'

'Sorry. Wasn't old enough for the Balkan Wars.'

I told the pilot to keep over the sea well south of the three peninsulas of Chalcidice and I would then give him further orders. When the three easily recognizable points were passed, I ordered, 'North-west and leave Mount Olympus to port!'

But three or four mountain tops were poking through light cloud and, as a complete amateur in aerial navigation, I could not tell which was Olympus. The pilot knew it, sneaked off too far to the north and tried to persuade me that the Vardar was the Aliakmon. Possible landing grounds were more likely in the broad valley of the Vardar but it was far too close to Salonica. I dithered until cloud-gathering Zeus went into action and blew them away. There, now behind us, was unmistakable Olympus.

I shoved the muzzle in the back of his neck and he banked to port so violently that he probably meant me to lose my balance, in which case the imperturbable Turkish general might come to his aid. The only result was that I accidentally pressed the trigger and had the luck to hit the windscreen not the pilot. That put an end to any tricks. Olympus and the Aliakmon were clear but anything flat enough to land on was not. The pilot came down, explored and chose a cultured strip of corn. We crashed through the young stems and demolished a vineyard, coming to rest with one wing well dug in and the tail in the air.

Beyond bruises none of us was hurt. Better still, no troops were in sight and the only visible road was a rutted track. The mountains sparkled where bare rock caught the midday sun and here and there were dark ravines like the stripes on a tiger from which another tiger could observe his prey. Men were running out from a white village about a mile off to see what damage we had done to ourselves and the crops – the crops being the more important in view of the shortage of food in conquered Greece. The pilot had no fear of them, aware that Greek villagers knew very well what would happen to them if a German was attacked. The general was none too certain of his status. He remarked that if a Turk were present at any disaster the Greeks could be trusted to put the blame on him.

I saw that there was no reason why he should be recognized as a Turk if he remained bare-headed and ripped off his flashy epaulettes.

'For the moment let us both be British,' I suggested. 'We have some proof' – I pointed to the dead guard, whose face, owing to the angle of the plane, seemed to be looking through the window – 'A pity he is not in uniform!'

'Which uniform would he be wearing?'

'Black. The Gestapo.'

'And you were his prisoner?'

'On the way to the firing squad.'

'I did notice that you spoke English without a trace of a German accent. Well, I'll do as you say. At least we shall be sure of lunch and a glass of wine while I wait for rescue. The Greeks learned hospitality from us. But suppose they insist on holding me?'

By this time we were surrounded by a band of cautious but very angry Greeks demanding compensation for the damage. In my inadequate Greek, I assured them they would get it so long as they treated the pilot with courtesy.

'And the British officer?' one asked. 'Did he kill that man?'

'I killed him.'

'And you also are British?'

When I replied that I was, there was great excitement. They forgot all about the crops and wanted to show us the way to the sea at once.

'But the pilot is German. You'll need him alive to explain to the soldiers what happened.'

I managed to produce a mangled and incredible story that the British officer was a prisoner on parole and that it was against his honour to try to escape. This resulted in a further wave of admiration for the British. I repeated it to the general, telling him that I was off to the mountains of Macedonia and he could be quite certain of lunch. He shook my hand warmly and hoped we would meet again.

'Shan't ask you to return my revolver,' he said. 'Trust you'll find it not so poorly balanced after all. Just a way of showing my neutrality. I wish Hitler's Reich was at the bottom of hell. On the other hand Russia is our hereditary enemy. And look here, old man! You're going to need this and I can always complain you pinched it.'

He shoved into my pocket a mixed wad of German marks and Greek drachmae.

'Just a way of saying thank you for London in the nineteen-thirties and all those splendid messes where I was entertained. I was then assistant military attaché ...'

Two of the villagers took me straight up into the mountains after I had threatened them with my revolver, so that both pilot and general, in genial mood after goat's milk cheese and the local wine, could swear they had not given me willing assistance.

My guides set out to take me up the Aliakmon and on to high ground from which I could pick out the landmarks which would lead me round Mount Olympus to the sea. Every Greek on meeting some survivor of the British defeat a year earlier assumed that he wanted to reach the sea. As soon as I reasonably could, I sent them back to their village, telling them to say they had escaped from me and, if threatened with any violent method of interrogation, to tell the truth. Having thus left a false trail for any search party, I turned back to the Aliakmon, where towards evening I found myself among the remains of mounds and trenches. Whether they dated from this war or the last I did not know, but the derelict defences offered a night's lodging.

The air was warm and carried scents of the herbs of Greece. I had no need to tuck the fleecy coat around me. I lay there considering what sort of damage a single man, carrying on his private war, could do to the enemy with no skills but those of the hunter and lone rover. When I made my despairing choice to risk the flight to Salonica, the mind's picture was romantic. It hadn't time to be much else. Food. Well, I had enough for two or three days. After that I could probably depend on villages and shepherds once the word had gone round that I was careful and trustworthy. Money. Enough for the present. Clothes. I couldn't go round in my Bucharest suit, but I could keep trousers or coat if sufficiently dirty and obtain a peasant's top or bottom in exchange. Arms. Four rounds in a .38 revolver was not much for a private war; I needed one of those military hosepipes but a rifle was infinitely preferable. Identity. Well, Private Bill Smith would do for local purposes. The passport in the name of Ludwig Weber might come in handy if presented to simple soldiery who rarely had dealings with the Gestapo. I also retained Haase's documents, though I would never again dare to use them except in extreme emergency.

A delightful thought upon which to close my eyes was of that not-so-secret office in Istanbul. When it was discovered that the major had been bluffed by the fake Haase into sending him to Salonica for identification, at the same time providing Turkish army messes with a good story at the expense of the SD, would an enraged Führer, never forgetting the narrow escape he had had, reduce him to the simple job of slaughtering civilians or stick him up against a wall?

When the sun was up I took stock of the unknown landscape. West of the river a range of mountains closed the horizon. They were very different to the high Carpathians with their steep, dark valleys where an armed band could disappear and defy pursuit. Here was rock under intensely blue sky and only low scrub for cover, all at the comfortable height of some four thousand feet. In such a canopy of light it seemed to me that to be safe an outlaw could be no larger than a rabbit. However, there were hints of precipice and gorge and for the present there was nowhere else to make my home.

First I had to cross the river. Down stream was a bridge with a steady flow of German military traffic. That relieved one of my fears: that I might find myself in a district garrisoned by Italians with whom I had no quarrel. It's a common misfortune for all nations to be governed at some time by a clown, especially if he turns out to be a belligerent clown. The bridge obviously would be heavily guarded, so there was nothing for it but an early morning plunge into the fast current, pushing ahead a piece of timber revetment with my clothes and my few possessions. Then I climbed up into what would be my hunting ground, hungrily eager to explore it and see what prey it might hold.

4

Villages were few, clinging to slopes like a scatter of nesting gulls, one house above another. For the first days I did not visit any of them and spent my time in search for my future headquarters, sometimes sleeping in shallow caves – if they were not occupied by goats – and sometimes in the thick scrub of the ridges. In places this scrub was so dense that if I burrowed into it well away from any path I could not be discovered unless stepped on. It swarmed with ticks and, while admirable shelter for the fugitive until danger had passed, it could not form a base for attack. One could see nothing without standing up.

My first contact was with a goatherd. When I had answered his questions and he had found out that I was British and on the run, his first reaction, typical of all of them, was to say without any regard for possible consequence, 'You must come to my house and we will have a party.'

I thanked him profusely as one gentleman to another and answered that I would gladly come to his house at night but there must not be any party. At some time I might have to kill and I refused to risk reprisals against them.

'They don't come up here much,' he said. 'Goats and hunger, that's all we have.'

'What troops are there in the district?'

'Many, many, at Kozani and on the roads.'

My territory was the range running north from the bend of the Aliakmon to Kastoria, with the town of Kozani on lower ground to the east. It seemed to be a crossroads of strategic importance, one running south from Macedonia to Athens over the Aliakmon bridge, the other to Salonica, so a garrison had to be there.

'And are there partisans to keep them busy?' I asked.

'No. All are over to the west. Here is nowhere for a band to retreat and be safe.'

Indeed there was not, but one man could vanish when a dozen couldn't. However, I did not ask him if he knew of a refuge for me. None of them could be allowed to know where I was.

'I hear an Englishman shot down an aeroplane by the river. Could that be you?' he asked.

Rumour had arrived, and with the same exaggeration as a press report. My reputation was safe.

I agreed to come to him after dark, and he led me along the ridge until we could look down on the roofs and I could single out his house and the path to it.

Privacy was hopeless from the start. This was the man who had shot down an aeroplane, and half a dozen males of the village were there to inspect him. They had little to eat beyond bread and cheese and garden produce, but in order that a party should be a party the goatherd laid on the table two precious tins of sardines abandoned the year before by the retreating British.

While on the subject, I asked whether the troops had left no arms behind them. No. It would have been possible to pick up a useful bit of this and that, but they had heard in time that houses were being searched, and if arms were found the village was burned to the ground.

All the rest of my needs were easily satisfied. I exchanged my too conspicuous coat for the pullover and waistcoat usually worn by the peasants and after argument was allowed to pay – in view of their needs – for a small store of food and wine which would keep me from hunger without ever lighting a fire. More food would be hidden in a crevice in the bare rock which they would show me, where I could collect it and leave any money I pleased.

When I went out into the night the goatherd came with me to set me on my way. The others wanted to come along too but he invited them to stay and keep on drinking as he would only go as far as the top of the ridge. I felt that he wanted to speak to me in private.

'I know where there are arms,' he whispered, 'but in front of them all I was ashamed to say.'

He told me that he had a brother who had fought gallantly against the Italians in Albania. Yes, he was no coward. But when his regiment was ordered back from the front to fight the Germans there was some disorder, for they were all worn out by the cold and the battles and no longer fit to meet tanks. So he had gone home, passing secretly by his brother's village on the way, burying his arms and uniform, and then returning to his fields as if he had never left them. A deserter, yes. And there was no need since a week later all had surrendered. Still, it was not a matter to be talked about. His brother had told him where the arms were buried – near a striped rock which they both knew.

The goatherd promised to show it to me next day, but I should not go with him as the place was not far from Kozani and a stranger might be suspected. In the afternoon I must watch from above where he went with his flock.

It was on the slope leading down to the Kozani road that I found the flock. There was no cover but rocks and obviously the arms could only be recovered at night. Lying still at the edge of an inadequate patch of myrtle, I watched the goats very slowly and obstinately eating their way down hill, occasionally shepherded by their owner. At last he stopped by a rounded rock. At that distance I could not see if it was in any way striped, but, by his gestures and his face turned up to the crest where I was, he identified it for me.

It was as well that I had not accompanied him. Evidently he was nearer to the road than he had any right to be. A motor-cyclist suddenly appeared round a bend in the road, came weaving and bumping up the slope, dismounted and appeared to be storming at the goatherd with threats and questions. The black-uniformed brute then turned him round, gave him a kick up the backside and waved him back up the hill. For good measure he drew his Luger and shot the leader of the herd.

I waited till after sunset. In the failing light that striped rock was harder to find than I thought, and I was beginning to think that I must risk going on with the search at dawn when I came across the body of the white goat. I had several times passed the striped rock but failed to recognize it. The vein of rust-red in the limestone was only an inch thick.

So far, so good. But why had that demoralized soldier, who at least had the sense to see that further resistance was use-less, hidden his rifle when he could just as well have thrown it away? Though myself no soldier, I understood him. I had experienced that hour of hopelessness when the only hope is that hope may return. Suppose there was a miracle? Sup-pose all the German armour fell into the Aliakmon? Then he could dig up uniform and arms and rejoin his unit as if an involuntary straggler on the march.

There was no sign of disturbed earth, but a little way down the slope was a jagged boulder with a band of soil a foot deep all round it showing that it had been dislodged and rolled after heavy winter rains. The track of the fast freshet was plain enough but the cavity from which the boulder had come was not. A dead bush with new green shoots at the bottom was suspicious. It might have been planted to fill up and conceal the hole which was already there to tempt the soldier when he passed it. A tug pulled out the bush. Below were some flat stones lying on top of a uniform coat. Under the coat was a rifle and, apart from it, the rusty bayonet which had shaped the hole to fit.

Bolt and magazine were a bit rusty but the rest of the rifle was well oiled, proving that the deserter had been trained to take care of his weapons and that I had been right in my guess that he still could dream of marching as a hero through the streets of Athens. It was the old trustworthy British .303, as delivered by crateloads to any of His Majesty's allies who still had a use for it. I pulled it through, tested the trigger and loaded the magazine. The poor chap had been carrying plenty for use on the Italians; and there was no reason why it should have deteriorated.

I was now, I fear, a little irresponsible, but I was bitter at being chased across half Europe with no chance to do anything but snap back at the pursuit like a wolf with its tail between its legs. Where was my private war? Attack! I wanted to turn to the attack. To start with there seemed no more worthy target than the murderer of that harmless goat.

The motorcyclist had come from behind a spur which ran down from the ridge to the road. Under a half-moon – yet bright enough in the sky of Greece to throw shadows – it was easy to traverse the slope and reach the spur. Once on the top I could see the lights of Kozani and make out a small blockhouse by the side of the road below me, which was presumably the quarters of the patrol. Beneath the roof were wide slits showing light. Quite unconcerned, they were within and possibly drinking, for one of them went out to a field latrine leaving the door open behind him.

I would have liked a touch of white on the foresight, although the standing figure was fairly clear against the cement of the blockhouse behind him. There was nothing wrong with the ammunition. My first shot scored on the concrete, for range and my altitude were hard to guess. My second got him. Two of the guards incautiously dashed out to see what on earth was going on in this place of peace and passing transport. They never did see. Then a machine-gun started up from the embrasure under the roof, firing at the flashes, or perhaps – if the gunner had keen night sight – at my prostrate figure on pale gravel. He would certainly have bagged me if I had not dived for the shelter of a handy rock. He even managed to knock the top off that.

The gunner seemed to be the last of them, for nobody came out to try an attack on foot. I crawled along the slope of the spur out of that too accurate line of fire and round to the door which he had had time to shut. On the next occasion when he thought he saw something and loosed off into darkness, drowning all other noise, I tried the door, which swung open at a touch. He and his gun were on a raised platform and he was staring intently into the night. This time I used the general's revolver.

Complete triumph. A little unsporting perhaps, but no more so than when the lone hunter is after other dangerous game. It was plain now that the goatherd had for my sake taken the risk of pasturing his flock in forbidden territory, and that as soon as the four bodies were discovered the village and its kindly inhabitants would be annihilated. I had to keep suspicion away from them. Experience offered a fair parallel. When you have collected the remains of a man-eater's kill, you will find – if in any doubt – the trademark of the killer, and you will know whether he or she is resident or has padded for many hungry miles from some faraway district. The same principle applied. I would leave my trademark, and perhaps repeat it in future.

There was an official logbook in the blockhouse. I tore off four pages and wrote on each in German:

MIT COMPLIMENTEN VON EINEM UNTERMENSCH ZUM HERRENVOLK

Hard to translate into English because, thank God, the conception of '*Untermensch*' has never occurred to us. Perhaps 'degenerate' will do, which for the Nazis included Jews, Poles, Russians, other Slavs and, if they had not been allies, probably Italians.

I took four table knives and pinned the notice to the throat of each of my victims, having of course, in the regrettable manner of the Voevod, ensured that they were dead. The relief force could not possibly hold the villagers responsible, for none of them could speak German, let alone write it. The investigators of the SD might think that they had carelessly left a Jew free and alive in Salonica.

There must have been a field telephone or radio in the blockhouse, for I could hear the rumble of troop-carriers coming out along the road and just make out their low, fast-moving bulk. Again, what an advantage to be alone! By the time the men were out of their vehicles and saturating rock and scrub, I was off the spur and on top of the ridge. I could not see what was happening but my ears told me that the troop-carriers had reached the high ground by some sort of mule path. It was unwise to trust my luck any further. I must change my hunting ground like any other carnivore.

For the rest of the night I travelled slowly west until stopped by the deep and narrow gorge of the Aliakmon. Dawn revealed a savage country: a desert of ravines where only infantry could go, and goats would be limited to tiny green shoots sprouting from gravel. The gorge might do for a base if and when I decided to call off the battle, but it was too far from Kozani for observation and attack.

Short of any military experience, I could not prophesy how the enemy would react to a mere flea in their pants. All I knew was a little of the north-west frontier of India, where a Pathan sniper among the rocks can cause a deal of annoyance to traffic on the road below him. The method of dealing with him was, I think, political – by bribing informers, and threatening or subsidizing chieftains. Encirclement or direct assault only produced a few empty cartridge cases on the ground where he had lain. It was likely that such subtleties would be beyond the Herrenvolk and that I must at some period expect a massive drive by angry troops with nothing else to do.

For three days I stayed close to the gorge of the Aliakmon to allow excitement to die down, and after secretly picking up some food retraced my steps to the escarpment overlooking the road. There was plenty of moving traffic but pot shots at that range would be largely a waste of ammunition, so when darkness closed down I decided to have a look at the movements of game in Kozani. I hid my rifle in a dry culvert, keeping the bayonet stuck into my belt under the sheepskin coat. There was then nothing in my appearance to distinguish me from any other villager visiting the town.

As soon as I was in the outer streets, I noticed that they were empty except for the occasional patrol. A curfew. I hadn't thought of that. The centre of the town was un-approachable, so I set out like a stray cat exploring dustbins on a stealthy circuit of the fields, gardens and lanes of the outskirts, always leaving myself a way of retreat.

Romance. Disguise. The secret agent always in danger. The enemy was just as impressed by all that nonsense as any other simple soldiery: even my interrogators had given way to remarkable imagination. When I saw a casual pair of military police coming importantly down the street, more to ensure that patrols were doing their job than to arrest curfew-breakers, I took the risk of going boldly to meet them. If the audacity didn't come off, I assumed that I should be quicker on the draw with the general's revolver – an assumption which appeared optimistic as soon as they ordered me to put my hands up.

What really did the trick was a cultured German voice coming from a dirty, dishevelled Greek peasant with a week's beard. I explained that I had reached Kozani at the risk of my life, having escaped from partisans whose agents must never be allowed to recognize me, and that I must at once find and report to the headquarters of the Sicherheitsdienst. I then pulled out Haase's comprehensive pass and asked the sergeant to look at it carefully. When he saw the stamps and signatures, damned if he didn't salute! He wanted to escort me at once to the office of the Sicherheitsdienst. No, I said, one never knew who might be watching and my orders were to hide my identity at all costs.

'But, sir, you'll never get there. You'll be arrested at once in the main street,' he said. 'I tell you what we will do if you approve. We will escort you as if you were our prisoner and when you are inside the barracks you can show your authority and reach the right man.'

He handed back Haase's all-embracing papers and saluted again.

There was no way out. I might be able to bluff my way past any sentry, but after that I hadn't a hope. Gestapo and SD, so near to Salonica, would know all about the fake Haase.

I was smartly marched through the centre of Kozani and a little way out on the eastern side.

'There you are, sir!'

We had stopped opposite a Greek barracks, commandeered by the garrison. Fronting the street was a blank wall, pierced by an archway with two sentries on it. Through the arch I could see the parade ground and the main building. I cursed my impulsive folly. Once through that archway I should never leave it again, unless they were pleased to shoot me somewhere else.

'The office of the Sicherheitsdienst is in the left wing, sir. I believe there is a private entrance on the side street.'

I was thankful for that, though it might mean only a minute's respite. The SD preferred private entrances, which were good for morale. Decent troops were likely to be shocked by sights and sounds.

I told him to take me round to the private entrance.

'And give me your names if you have a bit of paper. I should like to report your tact and common sense. Heil Hitler!'

The sergeant cheerfully wrote them down. Poor devil, he would not have been so cheerful if he had known why I needed the bit of paper – should the opportunity arise.

Not a hope of escape. No lane, garden or shadowed corner. I had to enter that building. I signalled to the two military police that they could clear off now, and loudly knocked.

The door was opened by a Gestapo corporal with his hosepipe at the ready who looked at me with astonishment. I must be something out of the ordinary to have got so far through the empty streets of the curfew. Behind him was a long passage, with half a dozen doors all shut.

'Your pass!' he demanded.

'The captain, please, and at once. I will wait here.'

Again the cultured voice and the air of confidence did the trick. He turned about smartly with his back to me.

I leaped on him. My difficulty, I remember, was to stop him falling with a crash and at the same time to keep a hand over his mouth while twisting the bayonet. Perhaps assassins have a technique for that. He was quite dead. I had no time to pin my trademark, so I stuck it into his mouth.

Brutal. But this was war; and cold steel has always been an exaltation of war, though the sabre and lance cause viler wounds than any but shell splinters. True, a stab in the back can hardly be included in such cruel gallantry, but when the enemy is as despicable as the Gestapo?

All was so quick that when I opened the door and looked out my military police were still in the street. I had to wait till they were round the corner – an interminable wait, though probably not more than thirty seconds. Anyone might come down the passage or out of one of those closed doors. As soon as the pair were out of sight, I quietly shut the front door and walked away, exposed in a straight empty street. Down the first intersection was a patrol which challenged me, but was too far away to catch up. I ran and on my left passed a small builder's yard, for which I thanked God – not because I intended to hide in it but because, if I were out of sight, the patrol was sure to stop and search it. Just in time I charged at random into one of the narrow, cobbled Greek lanes where darkness and the slight slope hid me. No following steps echoed behind as I left the blank walls and wandered through little olive groves and over walled terraces, the outline of hills against the stars showing me that I had come out of Kozani on the right side. When at last I stumbled into the usual patch of thick scrub, I burrowed into it to get my breath back.

At first light I crossed the main road and after making a detour to recover my rifle climbed up into my home territory. Now, with the leisure to move about and look down, I had the impression that the full force of a furious garrison had turned out. They had no solid evidence that I was or had been on the edge of the range – I might be anywhere – but they did know that I had attacked the blockhouse from the spur above it, that I had shot the motorcyclist only a mile to the south and that I had entered Kozani by the western road.

The blockhouse was occupied; two troop-carriers were weaving up the spur and nearly on a level with me and, worst of all, there was a company of men who behaved like experienced mountain troops traversing the slope towards me and beating as they went. If I was going to show myself at all, it had to be now, before the advancing screen got within range. They were tied up in all that squat thicket while I was on rock and gravel with a clear scramble to the summit ridge. A few wild shots were fired at me, but I was soon over the edge and out of sight. The line changed direction, their left going hard for the top, their right traversing the slope obliquely to catch me if I turned back.

I knew infantry could never overtake me if I went straight on towards the west, but I distrusted the troop-carriers. I had already seen how fast they could pick their ground. The best way to get clear was to go north into country I hardly knew, round a low peak carved and riven as if by a mad Gothic architect, and into the surrounding bare, broken crags where troop-carriers could not follow and there was plenty of cover in which the advancing line could waste their time searching for me. The whole enemy screen was now behind me, leaving piquets on the edge of the range in case I dashed down in the direction of Kozani. Sometimes they had a chance of a harmless snapshot, as likely as not taken standing awkwardly on one leg.

As I thought, the carriers could not take the crags and remained on a track which wound along the eastern slope, cutting me off from the low ground but nowhere else. I had time in hand to try a little north-west-frontier stuff on the nearest carrier, scoring on a too eager head-and-shoulders. The response was efficient and immediate. Something loudly exploded twenty yards behind me. It was my first experience of a mortar – evidently a useful weapon for keeping a sniper on the move.

The spurt of splintered rock at least pinpointed my position for the following line. I was not sorry for that, since the direction of their attack was clear. So far as I could see, they meant to sweep round the jagged cathedral of rock in roughly crescent formation and drive me on to the machine-guns of the carriers. That gave me time to fall back northwards using every angle and pinnacle of cover till I was somewhere beyond and outside the point where the left horn of the crescent of beaters ought to finish up.

They were still certain that I was inside the cordon and bound to show myself in order to escape. In fact I was already outside, having anticipated the attack and encouraged it to come more or less as it did. I wanted to be able to pick a single man, far enough away from his comrades for me to have a moment to label him with my compliments. I reckoned that this contemptuous insult would make them lose their tempers and conduct the search for me in such a good Teutonic mood of hysterical anger that they omitted military precautions.

It didn't work out quite as I intended. The pack following me were dodging about fairly close together. However, the infantry deployed from the nearest carrier were loosely extending the western horn, leaving two men behind to keep contact between the parties or perhaps close a gap. One of these men – he may not have realized how daring he was – had nipped swiftly into good cover and I was not sure exactly where he was.

It was easy enough to leave my own clump of rocks unseen

but then I had to locate him. He knew his job and if it had not been that a single clink of the barrel on stone gave him away he would have cut me in half with his machine pistol. Very slowly I crawled round behind him using all the old teachings of professional hunters. It was curious to see his reactions. I had not given my presence away by any footstep or rolling stone, yet he was aware of my presence, continually looking behind him and fidgeting. How well I know that sense of being stalked! An animal bolts, but a man, unused to the saving instincts of the preyed upon, accuses himself of nerves, cowardice, superstition. I knew what he was vaguely dreading as if I had been alongside.

At any time now I could have shot him, but that was not what I wanted. Nearer and nearer I crawled until there was only a little gravelly ridge between me and his feet. To cross it I could not help being heard. We jumped up together, but, as he had to swing round on me and I dived straight from the balls of my toes, the bayonet took him under his left arm with all the weight of my body behind it. There was no need to finish him off. A fine splinter of stone pinned the label to his throat.

Our heads must have been seen but probably no more. The mortar tried again, scored a near miss and I was gone. The crescent, so far as I could reconstruct it by the blasts of fire, became a flitting, stalking circle around the dead man, which made it easy for me to put the rocky summit between myself and this expeditionary force better fitted to engage a whole commando than one man. The way to the north was open, and soon I could proceed safely at a jog trot. When I reached kinder country I was utterly exhausted. There was cover of some sort. What it was I do not remember. I rolled into it and slept.

I was awakened by the distant noise of a tracked vehicle. It was far away on an even slope running down to the plain. It didn't bother me. I had no doubt that the search for the nightmare killer would go on, and by the process of elimination the enemy could be fairly sure in what part of the range he was to be found. The urgent problem was going to be food. For drink I could depend on the gully puddles or occasional springs among the rocks clear enough for any nymph. I ate my last scrap of cheese and stale bread for breakfast and lay down to bask in the sun with my hands behind my head, thinking not so much of my next move as of what my true objective ought to be. Ever since the plane hit ground in the eastern valley of the Aliakmon it seemed to me that action had usually been decided at half an hour's notice. It had been mere luck that I had been able to turn from badly wanted fugitive to the attack.

To return to the Kozani area would be folly; on the other hand, it was a pity not to exploit my minor military success. To continue vengeance, unremitting vengeance, or to disengage and escape to the coast? The second alternative was perhaps my duty. I could serve Europe to rid itself of this evil plague much better in the armed forces than on my own. Yet my private operations had been effective and to the bloodshed I had added political warfare. I won't say that my labels would have had much effect on the decent man in the ranks, but they might make him understand that respect for the Herrenvolk was far from general and that a plain, skilful, patriotic soldier had been sacrificed from sheer hatred.

I set out to explore my new territory. The range was narrower with more plentiful stands of pine. A small lake was in the distance, and the hollows were marshy, one or two of them looking as treacherous as Dartmoor bogs. Evidently water from the winter snows of Pindus had difficulty in flowing down to the plain. The country gave an impression of emptiness, villages being far away from each other and tending to hug the flanks of the range. From the high ground, olive green in calm, silver in a breeze, one could see for miles. I picked out two troop-carriers full of black-uniformed Gestapo apparently doing a round of the villages to question and threaten. There was also a party on foot working the western side of the mountains. For the sake of the local inhabitants I left them alone. To kill one or two at long range would only increase fear and anger which they would take out on the villagers.

In the evening, when my hunters had packed up and gone home, I risked the noise of a shot and bagged a hare. Grilled over a fire built in a cleft of the rocks, it gave me the first satisfying meal for several days, so that I was ready to explore a piece of the night and gain some mental picture of the tracks which led from one faint constellation of candlelight to another.

I had noticed during the afternoon that below me and a little north the tops of pines were showing and that near the edge of them a streak of red rock seen through the trunks could be the highest roof of a village hidden in the valley. It was worth investigation, partly for any chance of food, partly for its communications with the plain. To reach the straggling patch of woodland, threading a way in darkness between boulders and bushes, took a long time, but once arrived I found the trees well spaced and that I could walk silently over an even floor of pine needles – blindly as well as silently, for the stars were hidden and I had no guide but the slope.

When a distant, dimly lit window showed me that the village was not far below, it seemed to me that a cold finger touched my cheek. I stopped short, common sense telling me it was a dead animal, fantasy suggesting a kindly warning that I was about to step over a precipice. Putting out a tentative

143

hand I found that it was indeed a finger which had touched me and above it was an arm. A corpse, rags of clothing obscuring the outline, was hanging by its feet from a branch.

I waited by the body till the first glimmer of dawn to make sure what had happened and whether or not I was concerned. I was not quite alone, for nailed to the tree was an icon of St Michael, whose drawn sword kept watch over the dead or perhaps promised a day of reckoning. The body was striped like a zebra with dried blood, the clothes shredded by the whip. Did they believe that he had hidden me, or was this cruelty just a warning to an innocent village of what would happen to anyone who gave me help?

I stayed long enough to watch the black-veiled figures of two mourning women, his mother and his young wife, come out as soon as the light allowed accompanied by the priest. I gathered from their high voices a lamentation that they did not dare to cut him down; if he was not still there for the crows when the next detachment of the Gestapo passed, another would hang from the branch in his place. From then on, my self-questioning conscience knew no more feelings of guilt.

Very cautiously I returned to the summit where I could occasionally glimpse some of the hunting parties. By affixing my labels I had done my best not to involve the local inhabitants in the Kozani district, but here the Gestapo, determined to have victims, were following their usual practice of choosing them at random on the general principle that since everyone loathed them no one could be innocent. Movements of carriers and, where roads were passable, a few cars, suggested that they were trying to run me to earth by means of interrogation. Their exploration of the tops was perfunctory. After all it would have taken a line of men at five-yard intervals to flush me out, and there could not be troops to spare left in the mountains of Macedonia.

After observation for a whole day I became familiar with the few cross-country tracks, limited in their windings by cliff or woodland or marsh. If only, I thought, I could lay my hands on a mine and know how to arm it and bury it! I had not even a spade to dig a game trap, which I knew well how to disguise so that hippo or even elephant, sticking to the same path through forest or tall grass, fell into the straight-sided pit and were impaled, to be finished off by the broad-bladed spears on their way to the communal pots.

For the next day and night I was without food. Possibly I could have found a peasant to trust but after what I had seen I refused to involve any of them. The only hope of edible life was on the kinder slopes of the west of the range rolling down in waves and terraces where neither rocks nor scrub were tall enough to hide me. In daylight it was dangerous. A road crossed it halfway down with a fair amount of military traffic which sometimes put out patrols. The enemy had the same conviction as the Greeks: that an English fugitive would always make for the sea.

On the edge of one shallow depression, deep enough to hide me from the road, there were frogs about but too nimble to catch with my hands. As for a bullet, that would not leave me much of a frog even if I could hit it. Then I found a competitor also after frogs. It was a fine, fat snake good for two meals and easily to be captured if he didn't wriggle into a crack. He went fast for the nearest boulder and, as he was as fast as I over ankle-breaking ground, I started to run across a patch of dead grass in order to cut him off. In an instant I was up to the knees in bog and could never have got out if a clump of coarse grass had not been just within the reach of a stretched arm.

The snake was still catchable and I caught it. That success was enough for the moment and I hardly realized what a narrow escape I had had. However, before leaving for my wind-swept home and breakfast I had a close look at the extent of the bog so that I could avoid it in future. It was not very broad and formed a sort of tableland of its own, with the rough ground over which I had chased the snake on one side and a long rounded ridge on the other with occasional clumps of rushes and the same dead, matted grass as the rest of the hillside. The bog itself was a trifle greener, and I think I would have spotted it if I had not been concentrating on the snake.

That thought married up with my futile dreams of elephant traps. But the snake to be chased would have to be me, and there had to be an easy, tempting approach up from the road. I walked round the head of the bog and decided that the surface of the hillside should not give any trouble at all to a tracked vehicle. If the occupants caught sight of me – identifiable at once by the rifle slung on my back – above them, the right tactical approach was to leave the road, bounce over a couple of ridges, then go straight for the top and deploy as soon as the going became impossible. Don Ernesto, alias Captain Haase, alias Ludwig Weber, was doomed. The only snag was that he really might be.

Hunger could wait. Snake grilled can be excellent but a bite at snake raw was prohibitive. I chose a lair at the foot of the cliffs from which I could look down and command a mile of road. It was easy to spot me from above and I could only pray that none of the foot patrols, admittedly rare, would choose that morning for reconnaissance of the ridge.

I had to wait till the early evening for a worthy victim. No carriers passed, only country carts and a couple of staff cars. Then at last a troop-carrier full of black uniforms came in sight, travelling back to the south after some bestial outing. I started to attract their attention a little late, for it went against the grain to show myself openly after all this time of practising the stealthiness and camouflage of a leopard among rocks. Outlined against the cliff I moved along it turning over stones and poking into crevices as if desperately searching for something to eat. Even so it took them the hell of a time to notice the careless figure above them.

The carrier suddenly swerved off the road and went hard at the slope, making such a racket that I could no longer pretend not to have heard and seen it. They saw me dash for cover, fail to find it and run across a stretch of open grass in panic – a necessary pretence which was much too real for my comfort. I was now within easy range and their machine-gun opened up in spite of the swinging and lurching of the carrier; if they had stopped long enough for any man to take aim, he must have bagged me. But they charged straight up after this killer of the mountain all intoxicated by anger and mere speed, until the carrier flung itself over that gentle ridge.

I had now thankfully dropped flat behind the boulder where I had caught my snake, so that I was deprived of the joy of watching the disaster. When the firing had stopped and there was no louder noise than shoutings, alarms and frenzied advice, I looked out. The tracks were already under and threshing up mud until they stopped. The vehicle then visibly sank a couple of feet with its tail in the air. Two black uniforms had jumped out into the bog and were hanging on. The rest were fluttering up and down in their seats. As soon as the machine-gun was pointing into the green slime and personal weapons were no longer at the ready, some even thrown overboard to get rid of the weight, I could safely stroll out of cover and wish them good evening. They called for help, though it should have been quite obvious that there was nothing I could do or had any intention of doing. The carrier disappeared with men still standing on it up to their thighs. I left the trap and its victims. Even I did not wish to see any more.

It was necessary to leave a label. The tracks of the carrier could show where it had left the road, and the white bullet marks on stone that it had given chase to something which had to be me; but I did not want the area commander to think that total submersion in the bog was pure accident. So I carried some of the thick black mud up to a smooth face of stone a little above the bog and drew a passable swastika with an arrow pointing at the centre. It was not wholly gratuitous insolence. As before, I wanted partly to protect the villagers and partly to add force to the morale-shaking myth which must be gathering about me.

The craggy, rugged top of the range was going to be too hot to hold me, so I decided to make for the gorge of the Aliakmon which I had inspected after my attack on the block-house, considering it a suitable hideout although too far away to take advantage of the alarm I must have caused in Kozani. I crossed the road intending to travel with caution during the remaining hours of daylight and after dark to make all possible speed along made paths. Hunger had returned after the anodyne of action. I looked forward to a bit of peace in which to eat my snake.

I reckoned that I had plenty of time to escape before any force set out from base to find out what had happened to the missing carrier. For a second time I had inexcusably forgotten radio. I suppose body and mind had become too thoroughly the timeless and predatory carnivore. I was only half a mile away when I saw a platoon of infantry deploying at the side of the road and rushing the slope to answer the desperate appeal of the vanished carrier. They could be certain that I had not gone far since I had wasted time painting in mud my contemptuous swastika.

In any case, I thought, they were bound to cordon the tops till every cleft and rabbit hole was searched. They could not know yet that I had crossed the road. Another wrong assumption. While I was trotting along a mule path at the bottom of a twisting valley with no cover on either side, a light plane swooped round the bend behind, unheard until it was nearly over me.

I could see woodland ahead but it was too late for sheltering pines to be of any use to me now. The enemy could have no doubt that I was heading for the gorge – not an easy crossing in any case and nearly impossible if parties were out on the banks and on the heights above. My position, trapped within the right-angled bend of the Aliakmon, was desperate. The only way out was round the head of the river by night marches and without a map. So far as I knew, that move would take me into Albania and more desolate ranges than any I had seen, where I could choose between capture or starvation. Even supposing I could reach the sea in one piece only the Italian coast was across the water. The best bet was to go to ground and allow the hounds to overrun me if I could manage it. I might then be able to see what dispositions they had made and cross the river in spite of them.

The immediate necessity was to reach the woodland, light a fire under cover of the thickest branches, and eat. In a mood of fatalism this I did. I dared not sleep but in fact the hunt never followed the valley where I had been spotted: a sure sign that they knew a better and more deadly route. Before dawn I set out to discover where they had gone and found myself in country quite different from the slopes of scrub above Kozani or the marshes and crags further north. Here the hills were rounded, bare and speckled with solitary bushes, like open umbrellas left out to dry on shingle, which would give cover from the air but none at all from the ground.

Since I had to reach an observation post, I climbed to a crest regardless of enemy eyes and got away with it. Once on the top, curled round the trunk of one of these bushes, I could gain some idea of the lie of the land. To the west the hills were lower and cut by steep ravines down which the water must flow to the gorge of the Aliakmon. There were glimpses of military activity on the far side of the wood where I had spent the night. They had reached it by another parallel valley, which meant that after receiving the report from the air they had hoped to cut me off as soon as I left the trees, instead of chasing me directly. It was fortunate that they had taken this second valley into which I now looked down and it explained why I had never been seen. Apparently I could stay under my umbrella as long as I liked, but I could leave it only at twilight. That being fated, I put in hours of much-needed sleep in the shade.

When the sun had gone down, I followed the crest westwards, for it ran evenly on and saved me from descending into the network of shallow ravines where my right way by the stars might be the wrong way by these lanes of the land. As the long ridge began to fall away, I proceeded very slowly and carefully, expecting that the enemy would be blocking this obvious route as well as the valleys. Eventually I found their post – five men tucked away in a hollow with two sentries on the edge. I was pleased to see the post so strongly held. This normally unimportant district of Kozani must have been calling for more troops. I suspect that the incentive was not my raid on the blockhouse nor the bogged carrier but the impudent assassination of the Gestapo doorman. Only the SD in blazing anger could have had enough influence to extract troops from Salonica and Thessaly.

I tested their nerves by silently shaking a bush. When the sentries spotted the foliage wavering against the moon, they dropped flat and alerted the post. In fact they were well protected against a sniper. If he could see the target so could they, and the inaccuracy of their hosepipe fire would be fully compensated by the quantity of it. But they had evidently heard all the myths about this half-human *Untermensch* who would stop and label his victims under the very noses of their comrades. I slipped peacefully past all the excitement and continued the descent.

It was now my turn to be frightened of a bullet in the back, mazed in this country which the enemy had seen in daylight and I had not. I did not dare to follow a watercourse, for that was what a fugitive bound for the river would be expected to do. I was forced to scramble and trip and make far too much noise while the soles of Hauptmann Haase's admirable boots were taking the worst pounding they had suffered since the retreat of the Voevod.

It was pointless to go on, and though the approaches to that damned gorge must be full of nooks and crannies I was unwilling to choose one without knowing whether it was next door to the bivouac of a detachment of troops. This was not a fantasy born of panic. A faint smell of cooking was coming down wind and so near that I could identify onion soup. The tantalizing scent came not in wafts but on a steady light wind. Over the ridge, though so much higher, there had been only a bit of a night breeze; so I guessed that I must have reached some sort of terrace actually within the walls of the gorge or so close to them that I was feeling the wind which followed the water.

First light showed that I had indeed passed through a crumbling upper wall, hardly perceptible in the dark, and was in a lizard's paradise of fissured stone, its cracks filled with low, green growth. Beyond this terrace was the sheer drop to the river. I had chosen a quite hopeless place in which to stop where I could be seen as soon as anyone walked near me. The sentries whose supper I had smelled were less than a hundred yards away, must have heard me and were, I assumed, only waiting for full dawn to take action. Far away on top of the first wall I could see two more posts. The officer command-ing the pursuit had a fine appreciation of geography. Whether I was following the crest or either of the two valleys, this stretch of the gorge was where I must come out.

There was no chance of examining the brink and seeing how far I must fall before I hit the water. In any case, if I survived, I should be a floating target. I could of course put up a fight – short, useless and with no guarantee of being killed. Their orders would certainly be to take me alive if possible to provide sport for the Gestapo. I unslung my rifle, intending to put a toe on the trigger and save them the trouble, yet I was ashamed of it. She, my love, had never been allowed a chance to kill herself.

I remember how conscious I was of her presence beyond the other great gorge of death. I remember the daydream in which I seemed to hear her say, 'Not till I am ready.' I could not understand the message if there was any. That in some sense I lived in her, that in some sense I was sacrificing to her, like any pious pagan, the blood of her executioners – all that was true, but we remain one person and so there can be no toe on the trigger then or now.

So much for the shadow world of a cornered, weary animal. Whether I ran or whether I humped like a caterpillar over dips and corrugations I could not avoid being seen. If only I could reach the brink, slip over and hit the water still alive, a sharpish bend in the gorge offered a wild, vague hope. When the current swept my body round the bend it would be a matter of minutes before anyone could get into position for a clear shot at me, especially if I remained close under the cliff.

Unaccountably I had not yet been heard. I supposed the slight rustle of my progress, which sounded like an earthquake to my anxious ears, might seem to anyone at a distance only a lizard and a falling pebble. But it turned out that there was another source of rustles. None of the post seemed inclined to walk my way even for a morning piddle. They were laughing, chatting and pleased with some diversion from the dull duties of watching the approaches. They had apparently confined something in a pit. Being plain, honest Württembergers, to judge by the accent, it was unlikely they would be mocking some imprisoned human being.

In the utter rock-bound silence I heard one of them say, 'We'll send it to the Führer with the compliments of the regiment.'

It would indeed have delighted the Führer if it had been 'him' not 'it'. What I could hear of the conversation then went more or less like this:

'He's in Russia, they say.'

'Well, there's always second-line transport from Salonica.'

'How are we going to get him out?'

'Same way as we dropped him in. Chuck a cape over him.'

'Beautiful chap, isn't he? Think it will heal?'

'I know the vet in Kozani if we go back that way.'

'I can't think how the sergeant had the heart to shoot him.'

'That damned townsman! He would!'

I was completely puzzled. A rock dove perhaps or a wildcat kitten? Soldiers of every nation are always ready to adopt a pet on which to expend the tenderness which the trade has compelled them to leave at home. And then I heard the unmistakable scream of a golden eagle. Well, not unmistakable, for this was a very angry eagle and only a nest robber would be familiar with that particular cry. It was too much to hope that the gift would reach the Führer and that he would uncrate it himself.

Evidently that trigger-happy townsman of a sergeant had winged the eagle, which had then walked some distance to the gorge, instinct perhaps leading it to try to take off from the cliff, and in the evening had come within reach of the post, more appreciative than the sergeant. They had captured it and dropped it into a crack from which it could not climb out.

'What about his breakfast? Throw him down some sausage!'

'Bet you he won't touch it!'

The whole party of four bent in a circle over that unseen hole in the ground. I crawled into a cleft just wide enough to take my body which I had been longing to reach ever since dawn. The next move, opening up a chance of temporary safety, was into a little sandy ravine which I had followed and then abandoned when I thought it was leading me in the wrong direction. I realized now that its lower course must go straight for the brink.

Apparently the eagle was out for vengeance not sausage. So several times had I been. One of the bolder spirits offered a tasty slice of hand. This called for application of a field dressing, prophecies of how many stitches would be wanted, whether the charge of a self-inflicted wound would stand up, and general confusion. I rolled into the ravine.

It did not end in a sheer drop. Winter rains had worn away the last few feet of the watercourse into a steep slope which I had to descend head-first in order to see what was below me and out to the sides. I was terrified of sliding over into the unknown and when, anchored by a foot in a crack, I was at last able to look into the gorge I was more terrified still. The river was low, and far beneath me was not water but a shelf of rock. After somehow managing to withdraw backwards I was shaking all over. The primeval fear of falling to death. Yet in front of a firing squad I should be calm and heroic, refusing to be blindfolded, etc. I have been near enough to know. I wonder if it works the other way round. Would these mountaineers who positively enjoy hanging on to nothing by fingers and toes be equally cool under a hail of machine-gun fire?

I reminded myself that at any rate nobody was at all likely to look for me where I was and stopped trembling. I could stay in the ravine till I rotted or the pursuit decided that I had slipped off north into Albania.

Heavy, determined footsteps crossed the ravine. The sergeant doing his rounds perhaps. An inspired guess. I could faintly hear the sound of raised voices, and then a pistol shot. Heavy footsteps and more of them returned across the ravine, and it was safe to raise a head. My four nature-loving Württembergers were under arrest. The sergeant – if it was he – carried under one arm the good Greek eagle, now a German corpse. For the moment it appeared that the post was not manned at all.

It was worth while to take a crawl round the vicinity though the temporary absence of any guard at that particular point was not going to help me to cross the Aliakmon. The sergeant and the four culprits were well on their way to one of the posts on the skyline, and relief sentries would probably appear very soon. I found the eagle had been confined at the bottom of a pot-hole just about deep enough to prevent it clambering out. I thanked its free spirit for the gift of the rejected sausage. They had also tried him with bits of bread, which were equally welcome.

Up to the present my view of my environment had been limited to some gravel and a clump of heather and all I had learned from a glance right and left out of that vile ravine was that the cliffs were sheer. I still dared not stand up but I had a few minutes of sunlit peace in which to consider my surroundings and think. Why had the posts been set where they were? The reason for two which I had spotted was obvious: simply higher ground. This one, however, did not on the face of it serve any useful purpose. I tried to put myself in the position of their intelligence officer in this desolate, sparsely inhabited district of Greece where till now there had been no need for a single German soldier; he would grab two or three villagers and ask them whether anyone ever crossed the gorge to attend christenings, weddings and funerals on the other side. The absence of any bridge showed that the general public had no interest. He would get the reply that of course there was a crossing which had been there since the days of Homer, Alexander, Lord Byron, or whoever the local hero was.

My intelligence officer would then put a neat circle on his map to mark the otherwise indistinguishable point where this murderous fugitive coming down from the hills could be expected to approach the gorge. However, it was far from easy to discover any route worth guarding on rock and gravel where no footmark showed and I dared not walk upright for a more comprehensive view. A mule dropping under my nose at last gave a clue to the path which ran across the terrace and then along the brink of the gorge.

Now all the beast needed was good cover where he could lie up till nightfall. A cavity in the rock, much like the eagle prison, was kind enough to allow one of the umbrella bushes to grow. Concealed beneath it, I watched through the leaves the arrival of the relieving sentries and when they had settled down to their duties felt safe enough to sleep. At least I was through the cordon. I did not look forward to traversing a sheer cliff in the dark but presumed that if a mule could manage it I could.

I set off by starlight. The path was just distinguishable and so was the emptiness on my left from which I was continually leaning away. It dipped down, passed over earth behind a neutral buttress standing out from the cliff and took to a ledge which had been widened by pick and chisel; even so, I felt that the mule which had tripped along it must have been somewhat undersized. There I waited till the rising moon revealed more of the chasm. I found that I was more than halfway down and that below me the river ran between a flat rock on my side and a stepped slope on the other. Myself I should have placed the guard post at the bottom and been wrong. From the ledge I could have picked the lot off with ease.

I cannot remember the rest of the path, which means that it must have been easier or that I do not want to remember. At any rate I arrived at the ford. A rope was slung between iron stanchions from bank to bank, for though the river was wider and shallower the speed of the current was still enough to sweep the wader off his feet. The other side – I thought of it as another land – was in no way alarming. The top of the cliff had at some time collapsed and the path zigzagged up among crags and debris.

I strode out along a well-worn path, determined to put as many miles as possible between the gorge and myself by dawn and feeling quite illogically a free man. As soon as heights could be discerned against the sky, I climbed the usual bare hillside and sat down to consider the next move. The country was broken but much lower, forming a cultivated vale between the range I had crossed and the forested foothills of the Pindus mountains.

It was another land into which I had come. I looked directly down on the village to which the path had been leading me, and could watch its normal morning life. There was something odd about the midday scene. Outside the tavern, civilians apparently on good terms with uniforms. They were not German uniforms. Only then did I remember that in the collapse of 1941 Albania and Epirus had been surrendered to the Italians, who could be expected to provide the military government and the occupying forces. Where the line between the two allies was drawn – if there was a definite line – I did not know. The only certainty was that the Herrenvolk had been left in complete control of all the vital communications between Athens and the Greater Reich.

I was conscious of an absolute blank in my knowledge of conditions. Ignorance was really no worse than at my arrival on the heights above Kozani, but since then I had become accustomed to a life not very different from that of a hunted man-eater, for whom the intelligence reports coming in through the five senses are enough. In order to escape or in self-defence I might have to kill Italians, but the overriding motive of revenge was no more. My private war was over.

Movement at night was useless and during the day presumably dangerous. My next objective had to be the forests on the slopes of Pindus, through which with luck I could travel south-west towards the coast, and my immediate requirements were food and friends. In the heat of the early afternoon when all was quiet I started. Dressed as the poorest of country Greeks, I could have passed unnoticed if it had not been for the rifle and a belt still fairly full of ammunition. As it was, I had to do my best to see before I was seen. I was several miles from the village and flitting from cover to cover when I came to a cottage so screened by tall and ancient olives that I did not see it until I was too close to retreat. An old man suddenly appeared from a straggle of vines climbing the olives like tropical lianas and hailed me: 'Come in quickly, friend!'

He was not in the least afraid of the rifle, seemed to accept it as proof of respectability. I followed him into the cottage and was formally presented to his wife.

'I bring you a true Greek, my lady,' he said. 'If I were thirty years younger, I would be with him in the mountains.'

'And getting yourself shot by Turks!' she retorted, having no use for heroics in husbands, but her own faultless, slightly oriental greetings to me also belonged to that period.

As soon as I opened my mouth, they realized I was not Greek and I introduced myself as English.

Welcome was more enthusiastic than ever and compliments flowed on my command of the language. Evidently I was one of the British left behind when the ships sailed away. How had I lived? Who had sheltered me? Had I joined the partisans? Had I wife and children?

Answers could not be attempted without further answers which would be exposed as highly improbable. So I took the easy way out and claimed to be a prisoner-of-war who had escaped with a stolen rifle on the way to Germany. Ouzo, olives, salads and cheese were placed before me while this admirable wife turned to set the stove with onions and a chunk of pork. Sheer heaven, yet the old man apologized because it was all they had.

In the course of the meal, wine and information flowed steadily. On seeing me armed, my host had naturally supposed that a band of partisans was nearby or that I was on my way to join them. Yes, partisans were in the mountains. The Italians seldom went out to engage them as they were so difficult to find, but if they entered a village and were given help it would be burned down. No, as invaders go, the Italians were not cruel. They had heard stories of the brutality of the Germans, but the Italians did not break into houses or shoot or torture; they had had enough of war and only wanted to be left in peace, though peace there would never be till Greece was free. And we, the noble British, had promised that it would be.

They assured me that I could stay under their roof as long as I pleased. That was the voice of hospitality rather than of common sense. I discovered that patrols did occasionally do the rounds of the remoter farms and villages, and that this cottage in the heart of its little paradise of fruit and fertility would be only a pile of ash if I were caught. So I replied that I would like to stay with them for ever but that it was my duty to join the partisans if I could find them.

In the cool of the evening I had a bath from the well, and after more wine the best bed. I thought that I should never get to sleep after so many nights on gravel or hard earth prickly with thorns from overhanging branches but the dark wine took effect and when I woke the birds were singing in the olives.

The old man was out. His wife told me that he had gone to the village to find out if there were any rumours of a stranger with a rifle. This was only partly true, but since they had so pressed me to stay with them indefinitely it would not have been polite to say that he had gone to find a guide who could escort me to the partisans. Returning for the midday meal with bread and salami, he approached the subject obliquely and told me that by coincidence a friend happened to be leaving for the mountains that very night and that if I really insisted on joining the partisans there might not be another chance for some time. When I did insist, he and his old wife showed every sign of regret and none of relief. Christian charity or, as my Turkish general claimed, the fine manners of the Moslem?

Dionysius, the friend, turned up after dark with three horses: two to be ridden and a pack horse carrying cheese and ammunition presumably stolen – if not bought – from the Italians. He was a real tough, brown and wrinkled as a walnut, and I felt he would prefer more proof that I was English than my word. For an escaped prisoner I should have looked filthier than I did. A sense of temporary return to civilization had induced me after my bath the previous night to trim my beard with scissors.

After speeches all round, we set off, travelling fast to get clear of inhabited areas. Dionysius was persistent in questioning me. I had been right to think him suspicious. I knew very little about the British campaign in Greece, but fortunately he was only familiar with the fighting against Italians on the Epirus front and I found I could safely invent arms, units and a last stand somewhere in Thessaly where I had been taken prisoner. He told me a lot about the partisans, stressing their ruthlessness and how they cut the throats of prisoners and spies. I asked if their leaders were men of education. Yes, army officers, he said, but good revolutionaries too.

We wound up through the forests and at dawn were high on a range far more barren than anything in the Carpathians, uncultivable and uninhabited. We rested ourselves and the horses out of the north wind – for the first time in Greece I felt cold – and while Dionysius snored I buried all Haase's papers under a stone with thanks and a word of regret. It seemed to me that there would be little chance of using them later on to impress the Italians, who had only to communicate with the nearest SD headquarters to get the truth; and, if I were searched on arrival by the guerillas, it was quite likely I would have my throat cut before I was halfway through my long story of how and where I became Haase. I could not count on there being no German-speaker among those revolutionary officers.

In the afternoon we reached the camp, admirably placed at

the foot of a hillock from the top of which a lookout would have a view over the tree tops to the distant open country. The camp was deserted, ashes and dung scattered. On the ground it could be spotted but probably not from the air. Dionysius explained that the band were always on the move, either because they had reason to suspect an attack or because they were preparing a raid and wished to lie up nearer to the objective.

We came upon the partisans at the head of the valley with a straight run down to a minor road which ran across the Pindus to the town of Yannina. They were about to attack an Italian post manned by a detachment of alpine troops who were becoming too skilful and well informed to be tolerated any longer. At first I was received with enthusiasm but then closely questioned by the leader. My account of the surrender of my unit was accepted and since I could not be caught out in my description of the country I said that I had escaped from the convoy of prisoners outside Kozani. Then what had I been doing for a whole year?

If I had come upon the partisans in the course of my personal war, I would have told a different story nearer to the truth and including my kills and labels, but I had already described myself as an escaped prisoner to the old couple who had received me and they had passed the fiction on to Dionysius. I had chosen it when too exhausted for much thought. I should have remembered that in Sweden it had once let me down.

The leader soon knew that I was lying. I was a deserter or a spy. But since I was English he would not have me executed there and then. My fate would be decided when they returned from the present operation. Meanwhile I should have to accompany them and my throat would be instantly cut if I attempted to escape. I thanked God that I had got rid of Haase's documents and that Ludwig Weber's passport was tucked away in the lining of a boot. However, he did not bother to search me, knowing, I expect, that such a castaway as I would have no papers, incriminating or not. My rifle and the general's revolver were confiscated and I was handed over to a partisan with a large knife in his belt and an unpleasant glint in his eyes.

In the late evening, when it was considered that the enemy would be more relaxed than at dawn, the band was within three hundred yards of the road post and apparently un-detected. A party charged straight for the Italian earthworks supported by covering fire which seemed to me an appalling waste of ammunition. I thought surprise was complete, for little fire came from the Italian defences. When it did come, it was from at least two heavy machine-guns out to the flank and well concealed in spite of bare ground. The Italians must have had warning of the coming attack. I had no doubt that if I were still present at the post mortem, which seemed unlikely, I should certainly be the first choice as spy or traitor.

During the very short and decisive engagement my guard was killed and I was lying as flat as a man can make himself. The Italians came cheering over the ground and the partisans faded away, having lost a good half of their number. I stood up with my hands raised and shouted that I was German, which at least I could prove – if allowed to – by the passport in the name of Ludwig Weber. The bayonet destined for my stomach wavered to one side, and what with surprise and a loose stone the man behind it tripped. I helped him to his feet without attempting to relieve him of his weapons, and he excitedly took his ally prisoner.

On my way to the commanding officer I had time to think up a story which could not easily be confuted. My immediate object was to avoid being shot out of hand – I had observed that no other prisoner had been taken – and to gain time. The Italian before whom they marched me was a pleasant young man who spoke fair German, not that it prejudiced him in my favour, rather the opposite. The imagination which had produced a brilliant defensive action was also inclined to ingenious fantasy.

I produced the Ludwig Weber passport and claimed to be an expert road engineer, a civilian employed in Turkey, who had been asked to report on possible sources of first-class road metal close to the main roads used by the army. A possible though unlikely appointment which could not easily be checked with the SD or army staff. I followed it up with convincing details of how I had been captured by partisans.

'Why did they not shoot you?'

'I persuaded them that I was British, an escaped prisoner-of-war, and some of them believed me. I speak good English and so did they.'

'But if you are German why did you join in the attack?'

'I had to. The alternative was to be tied to a tree till they returned. But may I point out that I was not bearing arms and surrendered at once. I could have killed your man who took me. He will confirm it.'

He summoned my captor, who did confirm exactly what had happened, and very sportingly added that we were out to the far flank near thick cover and that I had a good chance of getting away with the rest of the survivors.

'To whom did you report before entering the Italian zone?'

'I had no chance before the partisans grabbed me.'

'And you expect me to believe that you were sent out alone to collect road metal?'

'Only to report on the geology, sir.'

'Not on our troop movements and administration?'

'But I am a civilian.'

'Who can speak Greek.'

'A little.'

'You Germans are not as frank with your allies as you should be. We will see what Yannina headquarters has to say to you.'

To be suspected as an undercover German agent was an utterly unexpected turn. The only comfort was that it would take weeks of correspondence from army to army and department to department to find out who I really was.

Next day I was sent fifty miles down to Yannina in a returning ration truck. I was under guard, but there were points on the road where I could certainly have escaped if I had wanted to. But to what would it lead? More days of semi-starvation without arms and without any object. Yannina at any rate was nearer the sea, and since so far I had been accepted as German it was unlikely that I would be under close arrest. There was no reason for despair.

That night I was shut in a military cell but cordially treated, well fed and shaved. I became more confident that I could pass as a well-educated German wearing second-hand Greek garments to avoid drawing attention to myself. In the morning I was taken before a gross, sedentary staff officer content with his position and without any need to show two-fisted, virile cruelty in order to compensate for his fat. As he spoke no German and I no Italian, we settled on French. He started off by discussing the brilliant victory over the partisans, for which he undoubtedly intended to claim the credit. He went on quite genially to reproach my employers, not me, for imagining they could deceive Italians. His manners were excellent.

'You are not as frank with your allies as you should be, Mr Weber. If you will allow me to say so, you Germans are ruining Greece by your policies. It is we who will have to administer the country in the end and all you leave us is starvation and hatred. And now you send in agents to spy on us. Do tell me what you want to know! Whether we have more divisions to send to Libya to be massacred?'

I had no recent news of Africa. What I read in the papers before I left Berlin indicated that a large part of the Italian forces had been taken prisoner and that Germans would have to fight their battles for them. It was clear that the allies thoroughly disliked each other.

I assured him that my interest was geology not garrisons. The roads were breaking up and it was no use tipping in any old stone if the right sort could be found near at hand.

'Well, of course, Mr Weber, as a man of honour, you have to say that. But you have put me in a very difficult position.'

I had. It was embarrassing to return a spy to allies and he was too human to report an unknown Ludwig Weber killed in action as the SD would have done. He must also have felt uneasy about that German passport. In the sensible Italian manner, he decided that when in doubt shift the responsibility on to a superior officer. Orders were given that I should be shipped under open arrest to Taranto, where there was an intelligence centre with experience of foreign agents and closer liaison with interallied affairs.

I think the possibility that I might after all be British was not ignored; on the other hand, whether I was geologist or secret agent, the correct procedure was to hand me back to the German command with apologies and a courteous reminder that between allies there should be mutual trust. I was provided with a clean shirt and trousers and escorted down to Preveza, where a small transport was about to leave for Taranto with naval ratings going on leave and a few invalids from the army.

There were three more passengers of dubious antecedents. One was an Albanian who had been a court official of the deposed King Zog and was a member of the Italian administration. In conversation with him I gathered that he was a royalist and that he had become involved with so many rebels, patriots, Greeks and Croats that he had lost his way among his own intrigues. Another was a Jugoslav colonel whose activities were obscure, but he had to be treated with caution because he was related by marriage to Mussolini's mistress. The third was a slug-like official of the puppet Greek government in terror of his life even on board ship. He had, he told me, survived two attempts of partisans to assassinate him.

We four problem children were allowed the freedom of the poop but at night confined in a makeshift deck house, like a large chicken coop, at the stern. I was able to enjoy the smooth and shining passage across the Ionian Sea without too much brooding over the professional intelligence organization which would quickly discover all that I was not, but would have trouble in finding out from Istanbul exactly what I was.

On the first morning out, when we must have been about fifty miles south of the heel of Italy, we were waiting for breakfast to be served to us – since the ardently fascist captain refused to have such scoundrels at his table and we were too respectable to mess with the humble passengers – when we were tumbled into a heap by an almighty explosion. The chicken coop slid backwards and plunged into the sea. I anchored myself to the splintered door and the Greek grabbed hold of my ankle. When we came to the surface the Albanian turned up near to us on the planks of his bunk. The Jugoslav we never saw again. All that remained of the ship was the bow section evenly sliding under.

Our navy must have secretly mined one of the approaches to Taranto in the hope of sinking a battleship or cruiser, for the effect on our little transport of not more than three hundred tons was devastating. There were only a few bodies in the water and most of those mangled by the explosion. Little by little a few more, already drowned, came up from the depths. We three sitting on the shapeless roof of our deck house seemed to be the only survivors. The Greek was howling lamentations, though our raft was serviceable enough for the moment and he should have been singing. The Albanian with folded arms was playing the stern and silent mountaineer. I myself was coughing up water and already wondering what chance there was of being picked up by a British ship. I had assumed that as in former wars the Mediterranean was ours, not realizing the effect of aircraft taking off from Italy or that all our supplies and reinforcements for the Middle East were going round by the Cape for safety.

A section of the roof formed a sort of vault too low to tip us over but high enough to catch the gentle northerly breeze blowing down the Adriatic. My two companions hoped to hit the coast of Greece and knowing nothing whatever of the sea were continually trying to steer with a loose plank. The only result was to turn our raft in semicircles and I did not interfere, satisfied that to judge by the sun we were drifting steadily south and would miss Greece by a hundred miles.

There was no reason to lose hope. We were close to the sea lane between Italy and Africa and three times caught sight of ships on the horizon. I was not altogether sorry that they missed seeing us, leaving us to be picked up by that improbable British vessel which my ignorance of the current state of war had conjured up. After forty-eight hours without water, I'd have been glad to be picked up by a shipload of Gestapo.

We were at last spotted by a convoy bound for Tripoli from Brindisi. An oil tanker lowered a boat and took us on board. Officers and crew were all triumphant. A few more days and the victorious Italian army would be in Alexandria. Herr Ludwig Weber was astonished that they managed to forget Rommel and the Afrika Corps but did not protest. When we were some hours from the African coast our ship was detached from the convoy with orders to make the port of Benghazi at night. Depressing news for me. However the enemy disposed of me, there could be no chance of resuming my personal war. This Middle East which had beckoned me on all the way from Stettin now presented itself as an invincible enemy camp with no sign of my own countrymen beyond a plane which flew high over us after the convoy had dispersed.

There was not a light to be seen on ship or shore. We drove steadily for Benghazi, while unknown to us the slim, black messenger of death was sliding through the darkness on a parallel course, no doubt using the skilful cover of the seaman as I had used the skills of the hunter on land. The torpedo struck amidships. The effect was not so merciless as to our poor little transport, and there was time to observe panic. Boats and men plunged into a water where the calm and spreading gloss of the oil unnaturally reflected light. I jumped with the rest, determined to reach the destroyer, a dim outline behind the searchlight now playing over the hull.

Where the boats were floating and men reaching them without too much difficulty, they were left to get on with it; where survivors were oiled and helpless, the destroyer itself lowered a boat to help. There was, I suppose, no danger from enemy ships or aircraft, and the captain, who may himself have struggled in that emulsion like an oiled gull, could afford to be merciful. I avoided the tanker's boats, swimming directly to the destroyer and calling for help at last in my own dear language. I was home from my journey, or so I thought.

5

My passport in the name of Ludwig Weber had gone to the bottom with my boots, which saved me the trouble of destroying it. I was accepted on board as unquestionably British and gave my name as William Smith, a former resident of Italy who was being shifted from one internment camp to another. To have introduced myself under my true name might have resulted in being made free of the wardroom and overwhelmed with questions to which answers were better avoided until I reached land and the proper authorities. I had not forgotten memories of Sweden, which had remained dormant while week after week all my thoughts had been concentrated on vengeance and escape. It began to occur to me very vividly that now I should again be mercilessly hunted down by the hounds of wartime security and that in the end my only cover would be the truth, though unbelievable.

We were making for the port of Haifa. Why I did not know, and did not wish to be inquisitive. It may have been because enemy aircraft would expect us to run for Alexandria or because Haifa was convenient for disembarking enemy seamen. As soon as the destroyer docked, we were separated out on the quay. The Italians were loaded into army transport and removed. My companions, the Albanian and the Greek, were taken to the port offices and I was put up at a seamen's hostel, told that I should be wanted for questioning and that meanwhile I was at liberty to wander about the town.

As I had no money there was not much I could do. But

I needed none. It was satisfaction enough to walk among British troops, to observe Jews and their laughing children as carefree as in the London I left in 1938, and to exchange friendly greetings with Arabs to see how much of my Swahili could be understood. Then I walked up the winding road to the top of Mount Carmel and rejoiced in the view of this peaceful and prosperous land and of highlands which might well flow with milk and honey instead of the saw-toothed crags of Greece. Though neither Jew nor Arab, I was home again.

Home again. Had I any right to be? What home had she who should have been at my side? For more than three long years I had tried to avenge her, tried to play the part for which I was most fitted in the destruction of this evil as if I saw our tortured Europe in the image of her torn body. No, I had no right to peace. It was not here above the crystalline Mediterranean that I would find her. 'Not until I am ready,' she had seemed to tell me when I lay exposed and helpless on the brink of the Aliakmon. Not until she was ready had I any business with peace. Our union must come from some sacrifice in which her blood and mine were mingled, never to be separated.

On and on the trance wavered like a blown mist of the mind, but all I understood of it was that the mixing of the blood must be spiritual. How gladly I would have died if it could have been physical. Then I was startled back to reality. Someone had addressed me by name.

'Raymond. My dear chap! You look a bit down on your luck.'

There he was. A colonel. Probably handing out pay to the army, for all he knew about was money. A snob who always had made a point of being seen at the bar at our club on intimate terms with me.

'Nobody has set eyes on you for years. I was sure you'd have had your squadron by now. Where on earth have you been?'

'Shooting,' I replied.

He turned away in patriotic disgust, or more likely he was afraid I'd touch him for a loan.

I returned to my hostel and found an army sergeant waiting for me.

'Would you mind giving my commanding officer a little of your time?' he said.

The first approach of the British Gestapo. It was so comic that I couldn't help laughing and said I would be delighted.

I was driven down to a billet not far from the port where I was left waiting in a general office with cheerful NCOs coming and going and the occasional roar of a motorcycle beneath the window. Accommodation seemed rather more spartan than that of the Gestapo. I caught a glimpse of straw-filled palliasses on the floor of the next room, indicating that these special troops had no extra privileges, and of a neat little bar which suggested that the unit was civilized enough to be trusted with it.

I was led into the major's office. He sat behind a trestle table covered with an army blanket with two basket chairs opposite. The atmosphere was in no way threatening. I felt almost as if I had called to ask for a job with some tanned and travelled foreign correspondent. He had that sort of face, genial but politely sceptical.

'Don't they fix up distressed seamen with a new outfit?' was his first question.

'Perhaps I don't count as one, sir.'

'Well, I don't know their rules. There are so many kinds of distress in our world. I will see what I can do. Now, about your two companions – are they harmless?'

'Perfectly, neither are pro-Italian enough to work for them.'

'Oh, I wasn't thinking of that. But my obvious course is to hand them over to the Greek Brigade, and I want to be sure they won't meet with an unfortunate accident. That Albanian fellow – what are his politics?'

'Independence for Albania on Mondays and Tuesdays. Union with Greece for the rest of the week and when convenient.'

'I see. Just as you are Bill Smith on Mondays and Tuesdays but Ludwig Weber when convenient, or so I am told by your two companions.'

'A passport in that name was given to me by the German consulate in Istanbul.'

'And what is your true name?' he asked, accepting my reply without comment.

It was no good prevaricating if I wished to be accepted into one of the British services.

'Raymond Ingelram.'

'Borrowed perhaps?'

'Christened in St George's Chapel, October 1909.'

'Related to the royal family?'

'Not near enough to count. My mother was Austrian.'

'Why do you tell me that?'

'Because you will find it out anyway. I am also known to the enemy as Hauptmann Haase of the Sicherheitsdienst and Ernesto Menendez Peraza, citizen of Nicaragua.'

'Are you employed by any of our private armies? You can safely tell me.'

'Only by my own. I have fought the enemy for three years.'

He sat back, much more relaxed. He said that would be all for the present and suggested that I might like a check-up in hospital after my adventures. I replied that it was unnecessary.

I had been short of food in Greece before I was deported to Italy, but I was still physically very fit.

'Greece? You were left behind when the army got away?'

'I reached Greece through Poland, Romania and Turkey.'

'You said your mother was Austrian. I suppose it was natural that she had some sympathy for Hitler.'

'My mother is dead. She was descended from Kings of Bohemia. Is it likely that she would have even spoken to that scum?'

My anger must have impressed him as sane and genuine, for he gave up the idea of getting rid of me on to a psychiatrist.

'Who financed you in Germany?'

'I used my own money – what was left of it.'

'So you are well off?'

'No. I gave everything away in trust for my tenants before I left England.'

'Why did you do that?'

'Because I intended to assassinate Hitler.'

I could see that his doubts of my sanity returned.

'As an Englishman in Germany during the war?' he asked incredulously.

'Before the war. If I had succeeded and been caught, think of the repercussions!'

'But you seem to have returned and stayed on?'

'Yes, as a Nicaraguan. I was exposed but managed to escape.'

'Can you supply any evidence at all of your movements?'

I told him of my attempt in April to get home by way of Denmark to Sweden and how they accepted that I was British but suspected me of being an enemy agent, in which they were justified.

'I suppose the Foreign Office will have some record of

that,' he said, 'but it will take months to get it out of them. Anything else?'

'Have you any Poles here?'

'A whole brigade in training.'

'Ask their intelligence officer if he can get in touch with a guerilla leader known as the Voevod operating in the Carpathians. There is another in the villages east of Cracow known as Casimir. And there could be a Jew named Moshe Shapir who was a racehorse trainer in Germany and may have reached Palestine overland.'

'I will make inquiries. If your Shapir exists he probably arrived illegally, but that's a matter for civil police not for me. The Jewish Agency will tell me. Their intelligence service is remarkably efficient.'

'And today I ran into a Colonel Tracy who knew me well in London. But I would like him kept out of it if it is possible.'

'Why?'

'Because I have kept my true name secret. I do not want it disgraced.'

'It won't be if you have told the truth.'

'I must assume that nobody will believe I have told the truth.'

'Very well. For the time being I will ask the colonel to identify you and no more.'

'That is very kind.'

'We like to avoid publicity, Mr Bill Smith, until we have made up our minds what to do with you.'

'Deportation or the bug-house?'

'And you'll be bloody lucky if that's all, as a traitor to your country.'

'You know I am not.'

'I know nothing of the sort. But you don't seem the type to be a British fascist or a German agent. Now I shall arrange for you to stay on at the hostel and have a little pocket money. Keep your mouth shut, don't draw attention to yourself in any way, and report to my sergeant-major daily!'

So that was British interrogation. There were several essential questions which he had never put to me. For example: what was I doing in Istanbul and why had I gone off to Greece when I could have reached the British army overland? When the cheerful racket in my hostel dormitory had begun to die down and it was possible to think, I came to the conclusion that he had deliberately avoided questions which could be answered by a simple lie. They would be asked at a second, more ruthless interview after he had a general picture of the man and his movements which could found a sound basis for attack.

I then remembered that I had a very useful witness to my entry into Greece if he could be contacted; so when next day I reported to the sergeant-major I left a note for his commanding officer asking if it was possible through some Turkish representative to get in touch with Major-General Kurtbek, once assistant military attaché in London, who could state how Ludwig Weber entered Greece.

I was left alone for a week or more, my only contact outside the hostel being the sergeant-major, who knew of course that Bill Smith was highly suspect but found him a refreshing change from the daily routine of Jews, Arabs and straightforward breaches of security. He was the son of a Gloucestershire cattle dealer and had carried into the army the family gift for summing up a stranger at a glance. When he decided that, whatever I was now, I had been an honest West Countryman at some time, we could indulge in mutual homesickness and I was invited to take a drink at the bar. Kindliness or to loosen my tongue? A bit of both, I think.

'Men aren't what they were. Too many of them. That's the

trouble.' And he yarned away about the eccentric characters of his county loved by everyone who knew them.

This was a heaven-sent chance to find out what my world thought of me. I said I believed that at the other end of the county the Ingelrams owned a lot of land and were his sort of people.

'Ralph Ingelram! Now he was a wonderful fellow. I often heard my father speak of him. Killed on the Somme, he was. The best always go first, it's said. Married a foreign lady as if there weren't any beauties in London good enough for him. I reckon their only son took after her. Supposed to be the finest shot in Europe and always abroad. Now I'll tell you a funny thing about him. Just before the war he gave away all his possessions and disappeared. Some say he's in gaol with a long sentence and they let him use a false name. And there's a rumour that he's in Africa, but I don't believe it. He'd have beaten it back home to serve his country. Soldiers, most of them. One of them was at the taking of Jerusalem, and we know that's true because there's a tomb in the village church with his arms crossed like a crusader in his coat of mail and his sword at his side. Agincourt, too, they say. And the son fought for the Parliament while the father fought for King Charles.'

Pretty accurate. He left out my great-great-grandfather killed at Waterloo and the last of the line about to be disgraced as a traitor. Ah God! What sons my dark and lovely lioness might have given me!

On my next visit I was called in to see Major North – the skipper, as they called him. He was sterner than before and warned me that my only hope was to answer all questions frankly.

'Headquarters say that they have no facilities for dealing with you,' he said. 'And that as I have gone so far I might as well complete the preliminary inquiry. In the end you will have to be taken down to Cairo for the final word. You may go there now if you wish.'

I replied that I was very glad that he was to be in charge.

'Thank you. But we have a long way to go before you can be. Meanwhile here is some good news for you. General Kurtbek has given us a statement. He seems to be an admirer of yours. So is my sergeant-major. He's lost when it comes to foreigners. No languages. But I have a great respect for his snap judgement on any Englishman. Now I am going to take a most unusual course with an enemy agent,' he added smiling. 'Will you dine with me this evening?'

'As I am?'

'I can lend you a very natty civilian coat. We are about the same size.'

Himself in civilian clothes, Major North picked me up at the hostel and drove out along the coast to a little seaside town where we sat under a spreading Judas tree at a dimly lit table obviously meant for a loving couple.

Finding that my knowledge of current affairs had gaps, he put me at ease explaining the campaign in the Western Desert. He was certain that the enemy had got as near to Alexandria as they were ever going to, and would have the hell of a difficult retreat just as we had. His summary was very clear and I asked if he was a regular soldier.

'No, an amateur. I was a businessman in England. They picked me for a security officer because I spoke Arabic and German.'

He called for another bottle and I remarked that I had not been so well entertained since Berlin.

'Don't rush it! We'll come to that later. My impression is that Hauptmann Haase would be a good start. Tell me the whole story. I shall take a few notes but I am not going to interrupt.'

I gave him the bare bones of my personal war from Sweden and Rostock down to my surrender to the Italians in Greece.

'This burning hatred – it comes through. You never fired a shot without it. That makes the three years very hard to explain. Now let's go back to Berlin.'

I replied that it was easy to explain, provided he accepted that I had one idea: to kill Hitler. I failed, was caught, bestially interrogated, but managed to crawl back to England. I told him how they sent an assassin after me and how when I had killed him I took his Nicaraguan passport, which enabled me to return to Germany and try again. I was trapped in Berlin by the outbreak of war which I could have sworn our government was too timorous to declare. Then I conceived the idea of being a known and trusted Nazi propagandist in order to get near my victim. But I became sick of my own parodies and tried to get home. The rest he knew.

'No one will believe that you could have had such patience.'

'Do you?'

'Not on the evidence you have given me. Why did you label your dead?'

'To protect the villagers.'

'Did it? You never had time to find out. My sergeant-major has of course reported to me what you said to each other. The Ingelrams came up. Don't worry! I won't give your identity away till I have to. I accept your private crusade. But it does not sound like an Ingelram to label his dead. Why did you do it?'

'Subconscious reasons perhaps.'

'Subconscious, my backside! You've never fussed about your subconscious unless it was failing to warn you of trouble waiting behind the next bush. Why? You know the answer. Out with it!'

'Have you ever been in love?'

'Who hasn't?'

'I mean, so entirely that to both of you the two bodies and souls were one.'

'Near enough. We are married now.'

'And what would you do if the perfection that you loved had been tortured to death by these devils?'

'Suicide or the bottle.'

'No vengeance?'

'Vengeance is mine saith the Lord. And it's coming to him all right.'

'Now do you understand?'

'Understand, no. Believe, yes. At last it all makes sense. But I cannot make Cairo swallow a love story against the facts.'

'Is there any fact more absolute than love?'

'All the same I wish the Poles could have helped.'

'The Voevod?'

'His band has been wiped out. All they know is that it was infiltrated by the Sicherheitsdienst. I thought it best not to mention your stay with them.'

'And Moshe Shapir? Any luck?'

'I'm afraid he won't impress as a witness. He's doing ten years in Acre Gaol. He shot at an immigration official.'

I shouted that I couldn't believe it, that Moshe was so gentle.

'Then you see our trouble. With you as well. We are not equipped to deal with cases of monomania. Has it ever occurred to you that a fair translation of Herrenvolk is Chosen People?'

Moshe's crime was serious. He was one of a party of four who had travelled down through Turkey and Syria passing as Greeks from Istanbul on their way to join the Greek forces in Palestine. They tried to ride across the desert frontier but missed the way, ended up at a police post and were detained for questioning. Moshe, sure to have bagged the best horse, jumped the wire and galloped away. He was shot at, turned round in the saddle, shot back with an old Colt .45 and winged an immigration officer. God, what a fluke! And what a fool! He should have galloped on. His people would have spirited him away in no time.

I asked if it would be possible to question him.

'Yes. I have already got permission. It must be in my presence and that of a warder.'

I have written of several irreversible turning points in my outward and inward life. Memory is not clear enough to say whether I recognized them at the time. But of the effect of this meeting with Moshe I have no doubt. A cold and formidable place was that citadel of Acre. Well, Palestine then was threatened from north and south, but still the criminal was dealt with promptly, efficiently and by due process of law. Moshe was marched in to our presence by a warder who was alarmed when he broke away and threw himself into my arms.

'Ernesto!' he cried. 'Thank God you got through.'

I could only say the same and how distressed I had been by the deplorable story of his arrival in the land for which he had so longed.

'What does it matter? I am in Israel and I shall be free long before the ten years are up.'

'Quite likely,' the major murmured, 'providing Himmler doesn't get here first.'

'But you, Moshe! You who were so repelled by violence!'

'You taught me not to be.'

Volubly and with excited gestures which I had never before seen him use – stemming from childhood perhaps and long abandoned – he told our story, remembering little incidents which I had ignored or forgotten, his voice breaking with anger and indignation that a British agent could be thought a Nazi. But on all of it there was no conclusive proof. Of my life in Germany of course he knew nothing, nor could he confirm how I had come by the name of Ludwig Weber and why I had been specially flown to Salonica.

'Swear that you will come to see me and ride with me when Israel is ours,' he demanded.

I promised, though sure that within ten years he would never have the Israel of his dreams and that my own destiny was incalculable.

We returned to Haifa and he to his cell. All night Moshe's words haunted my weary brain like a recurring tune that one cannot dismiss: 'You taught me.'

Yes, by example over and over again. I had also justified unlimited violence. In that I was right when it came to war and the defence of our once sweet Europe. But private war? What sort of character would wade in blood and glory as I had done?

When I made next day my routine report, Major North told me that he had made a note of Moshe Shapir's evidence and added it to my dossier. We were now ready for Cairo's final judgement.

'Before we go,' he said, 'and while I am still in charge of your case, isn't there anything I can do for you?'

'Yes. Would it be possible for me to see Jerusalem?'

'A conducted tour or from far off like Richard Coeur de Lion?'

'From far off. In streets I am distracted by reality.'

'On collar and chain?'

He had put it well and I agreed. He said that he had to drive up to Jerusalem on a short visit to his colonel and that he would take me with him.

'I will leave you to yourself – on parole as they used to call it when wars were fought between gentlemen. Give me your word of honour that you will not try to escape!'

I gave it. In any case both of us knew that if I took to the hills it would be a confession of guilt.

The road to Jerusalem reminded me a little of Greece – the same scrub, the same rocks but all on a smaller scale, good enough country for ambush but not for refuge; an Arab would choose the desert for that, a Jew some settlement where he could be hidden and his identity disguised. I was ashamed to find myself thinking of the opportunities for an outlaw. This land was stern and calm as the religions it had fostered. Under the blue bowl of the watching sky one God was enough.

He stopped on the top of Mount Scopus, saying that he would be back in a couple of hours and pick me up by the roadside.

The great, grey block of the city lay below me, the tiles of the Mosque of Omar flaming in the sun. I had the impression of a fortress built and walled to contain the divine. But the unknown purpose cannot be visited through a door. It is in the open air that man and his fellow creatures, though themselves wordless, rejoice in the gift of life and movement and give thanks for the sense of unity which we call beauty.

Was this the view which fierce King Richard saw as he thrust his head and shoulders over the ridge, perhaps with my ancestor by his side, and after crying out that he was unworthy to approach withdrew to cover? It was an excuse. He knew his force could never take Jerusalem. But in excuses there can still be truth. I too could say I was unworthy because my crusade had come to its end.

Moshe's words were still an obsession: 'You taught me.'

I stretched out my arms to that enigmatic sky which canopied Jerusalem from hill to hill and swore an oath to myself – for what is self but a receptacle of Purpose – that never again would I fire a shot at man or beast. Emotional and perhaps absurd, since I know as well as anyone that man is the cruellest of all creatures and the bullet can be merciful. But I defend emotion. Even a snail must know emotion – either at the sight of a lettuce leaf or at the ripeness of one half to mate with the other – for emotion is the link between itself and other life.

When North returned, I thanked him for having chosen such a spot for me and asked him how he knew.

'I didn't, I just felt you might need a memory. Lord knows you have courage enough for fifty, but you may need a different kind of courage now.'

'Yes. I am going to be a different kind of outlaw.'

'You are ready to be told you are a supporter of National Socialism and a liar?'

'I have been through all that in Sweden.'

'Let's hope you won't have to again. But I have a reputation for believing fairy tales and they like to forget that once in a while I have been right.'

Early next morning we started down the coast road to Cairo, arriving at sunset when my body was delivered to a fellow security officer. On leaving, Major North presented me with his white coat and a tie, saying that he could not loose an enemy agent into the arena dressed as the shipwrecked Bill Smith. He cut short goodbyes, knowing, I think, as well as I, that no words could add to our strange and warm relationship.

Treatment was more military than at the seamen's hostel. It was also more comfortable. I was accommodated in a caravan fitted with all that a staff officer could need in the desert, yet there was a sentry outside. The combination revealed my anomalous position as a presumed traitor but also a thoroughbred out of the stud book about whose fate there might be awkward questions. If the authorities had known that no one was likely to ask they might not have been so cautious.

The house to which I was taken swarmed with officers and files. Passing between the ranks of the usual trestle tables and quick glances from the occupants, I was escorted into a private office. My interrogator was a brigadier and had a proper civilian desk; on it was a thick file marked RAYMOND INGELRAM followed by a string of aliases which I could not read. I disliked the brigadier at first sight. He had a dark moustache, more movie star than military, and a straight thin mouth beneath it, which seemed to carry a slight sneer as if I were an incompetent subordinate who thought too highly of himself. I judged him coldly efficient, the right man to deal with facts but, as North had said, not with a love story.

I remember little of that interview. It is not worth remembering. He started straightaway with the report from Sweden. I had claimed to be an escaped prisoner-of-war, but it was discovered that I had been in Germany as a civilian since the outbreak of war pretending to be Nicaraguan and that I had spent two years on propaganda directed at Latin America. I had claimed that my motive was to get near to Hitler in order to kill him. Did I wish to confirm that story? Yes, I did.

We then moved to my Austrian mother and the Austrian friends of my youth. To hell with such foolishness!

My escape. Well, there he had the evidence of the convict Shapir which was quite independent of my own. He was condescending enough to accept our stories.

'People in England seem to know very little about you. I have been able to obtain some newspaper cuttings which indicate that at one time your travels and your habit of hunting with the nets and weapons of natives caught the attention of the popular press.'

'They exaggerated.'

'Are you known to any of the East African governors?'

I gave him names, saying that all they could tell him was that I had been an agreeable dinner guest and had no political opinions whatever. I hoped, however, that if he approached them he would tell them that I was being vetted for possible service in Africa, not as a supporter of Hitler.

'You are suspected of worse than that, Mr Ingelram. You admit that you willingly allowed yourself to be employed in propaganda. I suggest that you tried to escape from the Reich before it was too late and to clear your name and your conscience by what you call a private war. Just how many of the enemy did you kill?'

I had to stop and think.

'I make it seventeen,' I said. 'That is not counting the Voevod's battle in the ravine and a truckful of troops drowned.'

It should have been eighteen. I had forgotten the stabbed doorman at Kozani, memory having censored him.

He was plainly shocked. I could see that he thought it close to murder. To him casualties were statistics. I doubt if he had ever been in action.

'Have you never ordered that a man be quietly shot?' I asked.

'That is entirely different.'

'Perhaps. But to kill a man face to face is not assassination. It only differs from bombing a town or wiping out fifty men with a machine-gun because you see his eyes.'

This was outside his experience and bad taste coming from a traitor. He quickly changed to politics and asked what mine were.

I replied that as a soldier – even in my private army – I was not supposed to have any.

'What are they anyway? I take it you have no use for democracy?'

'None whatever. It subjects us to government by a rabble of ambitious, self-important crooks. But even more, I detest dictatorship which adds fiendish cruelty to the same dishonesty.'

I had shocked him again, though he had probably said much the same about politicians in the mess. I meant to shock. Since I could see already that there was no hope of acquittal, nothing was to be lost if I disconcerted him by answering contempt with contempt.

He took refuge in a judicial air, saying that I would realize it was quite impossible to leave me at liberty. In Egypt, however, the only internment camps were for Italian civilians. So he would send me home to be confined or publicly disgraced with the rest of my aristocratic Nazi friends.

'What is your financial position? Major North tells me that you distributed all your possessions before leaving for Germany.'

'I did.'

'In order to tuck your assets away in Switzerland or Latin America, I presume.'

'No. But you may presume it.'

'In that case I will make a recommendation that you be repatriated at a minimum cost to public funds by any ship returning round the Cape. Do you agree?'

'I must, if your service insists on considering me a traitor.'

The following day he called me in again to tell me that I would be moved to Suez and very shortly embarked on a freighter leaving for England. No British passport would be issued but the master would carry in a sealed envelope the documentation enabling me to pass through immigration control into the hands of the police.

'And as you have no money, I shall provide you with a small sum for your expenses on the voyage.'

I thanked him and refused it, saying that Hitler's Ministry of Propaganda had paid me very well and placed funds at my disposal in London upon which I could draw.

A childish revenge. I had no doubt that Security and Censorship would waste a lot of time and energy trying to trace through what neutral country money had been transferred to London, how I intended to get at it and why in the end the traitor had confessed. North could have told them why. If an outlaw wishes to preserve his pride, he can only depend on himself.

I did not offer to shake hands on leaving, nor very properly did the brigadier.

I was decently treated when I went on board at Suez. Evidently the master had been told that he should keep a careful eye on me but not that I had been an enemy agent. He spared me questions, believing – so far as I could guess – that I was a person of some distinction who had committed some unforgivable folly such as seducing the King of Egypt's daughter or dancing a drunkard's jig in the cathedral.

The ship was to call at Mombasa, a port which I knew well, and there I proposed to leave it. I had never any intention of going home. My future did not matter. I had renounced the future and lived only in a past which contained, co-existing with me, the spectral vision of my love.

Somehow I could exist. Poland and Greece had proved that I could endure privation. But there could be no living off the rifle. 'You taught me,' poor Moshe had said. That lesson and my oath under the conscience-searching skies of Palestine were reinforced when the brigadier asked me how many of the enemy I had killed. Seventeen, I answered, omitting the uncounted. By what right had I killed? Was my justification self-defence or was it sheer anger and a savage eagerness to return blood for blood? But blood would not resurrect my beloved nor fetch from the void the children we might have had.

The captain did not object to me going ashore at Mombasa. He had no reason to suspect that I might disappear since I was on my way home and had no money. I had at first conceived the preposterous idea of walking to Nairobi. By now I was so used to using my feet that I hardly considered road or rail transport. How a white beggar would be treated I could guess: by the blacks with kindness, by the whites with an insistence on peremptory action to explain my poverty, which, if I were still close to Mombasa, must result in official inquiries and my return to the ship.

It was only when I had walked out of town along the railway track that it seriously occurred to me to take a train without a ticket. In a friendly, free and easy colonial society it should not be necessary to resort to the desperate tricks of American bums on the move. A freight train was halted hissing impatiently alongside a banana grove. I climbed into a truck half full of gravel and for the next three hours no one disturbed me. I was then discovered and rebuked, but merely advised that I should not be seen when getting off in the Nairobi yards.

It was early morning when I slid to the ground and walked away from my truck with, I hoped, the confident air of Hauptmann Haase at Auschwitz, though now my uniform was only three stained garments. I had to avoid the centre of the town in case some old acquaintance recognized Raymond Ingelram. I wondered what he would do: assume that this disreputable figure could not be me, or decide that it was and should be passed without a greeting. It was unlikely that in the yards I should meet anyone but merchants, white, black and

Indian, all busy loading lorries or cursing because expected goods had not arrived, so I sat down on a crate to watch them and speculate on their destinations. I did not care where I went, so long as it was not back to Mombasa and far enough into the interior for search for me to be abandoned.

The most hopeful prospect seemed to be an energetic little man with a face tanned darker than an Indian's by the equatorial sun who was loading crates which evidently contained parts of a motor boat to be reassembled on arrival. Some of the crates were marked in French as well as English, which indicated that the lorry must be bound for the Belgian side of the lakes. I asked the contractor if there was any chance of a job and told him some story which I have forgotten – in Africa all stories are possible – and that I had spent every cent I had to reach Nairobi from Mozambique.

'I speak French,' I added hopefully.

'And Swahili?'

To show that I was fluent I answered him in the language.

'You don't look as if you drank,' he said, half to himself.

'I have found better ways to waste money when I had some.'

'You'll have some if you can start this afternoon.'

Why do I record in detail this meeting with a stranger, having nothing in common with him but a taste for Africa? Because he set me on the way to peace. The mutations of a life do not necessarily spring from close associations but sometimes from a talk or a companionship which only lasts a matter of minutes. So it was here.

Why this record at all if it comes to that, considering Bill Smith is a non-person, an outlaw who renounced any steady stream of life as soon as it no longer contained love? Because I find myself unwilling to join those millions of other Bill Smiths who, as the Ecclesiast writes, are perished as though they had never been born. Then for whom do I write when I am the last of my line without sons or even an identity? For myself, I suppose. Here in the peace of the convent among these women who happily fulfil themselves in their duty to God and the neighbour, I spend the evenings re-living the action of the past – not wholly in repentance but, as it were, licking the blood from my whiskers with pride in the success of stalk and kill which relieves me of weighing right against wrong. I am content to be. I love, therefore I am. She had loved, therefore in some form she is.

My employer was an excellent mechanic and must have been a good picker of men, for his two Kikuyu boys, cook and driver's mate, were cheerful and intelligent. His navigation and choice of camp sites were poor, for this was the longest journey he had ever undertaken. With relief he soon handed over that side of the business to me. With whom and where, he asked, had I so much experience. Long ago, I replied, with a certain Raymond Ingelram of whom he had vaguely heard. He was disappointed because I would not shoot, but otherwise inclined to slap me on the back for every comfort of the wilds that I knew how to provide.

After delivery of our boat to a ferry company starting up on the shore of Lake Tanganyika, we made ready for the return to Nairobi. He was astonished when I insisted, in spite of his promises of prosperity for both of us, in staying where I was. I had to. The ship would have long since reported the disappearance of Ingelram from Mombasa and the Nairobi authorities, with so many old acquaintances to bear witness, could have no doubt of the real identity of Bill Smith. So my employer paid me off most generously and I settled down in Albertville for a few days until a Belgian mining engineer, attracted by the praises of my employer and the ferry company, appealed to me to take charge of his small safari.

He had no luck. As we were travelling up the Ruzizi River, I went down with a tropical fever which must have been rather more virulent than malaria against which I was pretty thoroughly salted. If he, not I, had been ill, I could have nursed him well enough to give him a fair chance, but he was inexperienced, in a hurry and afraid of fevers in general. So he deposited me in the nearest village, leaving one of his boys to serve me, under the supervision of the local witch doctor, who knew more of fevers than most consultants, but disliked the fuss and bother and questions that would result from the death of a white man. He put me in a hammock and two runners dropped the shivering bundle, like an unwanted baby, upon the steps of the nunnery thirty miles away, where it seemed to me in my fever dreams that white seagulls in a cloud were swooping over me.

They turned out to be the white robes of a heroic little group of Belgian nuns who combined a hutted hospital with farming of fruit, herbs and vegetables and a small herd of fly-proof cows – perhaps to remind them of the long-lost meadows of their home – where the grasslands began to merge into the forest. They soon had a Bill Smith in working order and then asked him where he wanted to go. I answered that I wanted to stay with them and serve them, requiring only my food and an outlying, watertight hut of my own. There were many tasks that a man could undertake for them more easily. The headman was a pious fool, always in and out of the little chapel and paying more attention to the candles than to the garden or the cows.

The mother superior asked me to swear that I was not a fugitive from justice. Leaving out the Gestapo, who had no interest in justice, and the brigadier, a limited man who could not do justice without papers, I could honestly swear that I was a fugitive from no one but myself.

'But why?'

'Because my love was killed.' I could not bring myself to tell her how, or of my vengeance.

'Yet you are so full of love to us and to the animals. Cannot you love God too?'

'I do. At dawn with birds and at evening with the beasts.'

She did not understand and was sad.

It is true that in the evening I join in the thanks offered up by the cries of the beasts around me. They have accepted me as of the same substance as these angels whom they do not fear. But there is one I wish had more fear. Killing is too easy for her. I have tried a dozen tricks to frighten her away, but she is impertinent like all cats. She knows me too well and I could swear she is jealous of the nuns. She has the white robes fluttering for the safety of the house, but with me in the last of the light she will exchange a quick, green glance as if there was some secret understanding between us.

Yesterday she jumped the enclosure and killed a cow. That cannot be permitted. Also I am a little afraid for the white robes; the margin between lack of respect and attack is so small. She has to die, my lioness of the twilight. I have forbidden myself to shoot, but there is still another way and in the Sudan I dared it successfully, hurled to the ground under my shield unhurt. One must provoke the direct charge, and I am not sure that charge she will. Another absolute essential is a strong shield of hippopotamus hide and a broad spear of steel forged by a skilled blacksmith. The headman has both in his hut, emblems of the past manhood of his tribe though he himself can't even handle a pitchfork properly. I must inspect them closely and see if they are up to the job. And then, my dear, the rest is up to you. If you will not charge, it cannot be done. If you will and I can hold the spear steady as you leap, the pain will be no more than that of the bullet.

Epilogue

When I was last in Kenya to stay with my brother, Sir Leander Harding, he told me that police headquarters had recently submitted to him most unexpected news of my old friend Raymond Ingelram.

I had learned after the war that, in the spring of 1942, Raymond had appealed to our embassy in Stockholm to get in touch with me, but Whitehall had replied to the inquiry that I was on service abroad and address unknown – the sad result of too much official secrecy and application to the wrong department. Since then there had been only silence.

Apparently, while being shipped home as a probable enemy agent by Secret Intelligence Middle East, Raymond had gone ashore at Mombasa and eluded a police search by plunging straight into the interior under the name of Bill Smith and settling down as handyman with a conventicle of Belgian nuns. When the Belgians withdrew from the Congo and the usual undiscriminating massacres began, the nuns were evacuated to Kenya with their insignificant possessions. Among them was a locked metal box which they had carefully preserved in the hope that it could be conveyed to some friend or relative of their dear Bill Smith. This they left in the charge of the chief of police. When still unclaimed after many years, it was opened and found to contain a pile of loose pages which revealed Smith's identity.

To his story I can only add that when the bodies were discovered the spear was through the heart of the lioness and her teeth had closed on his head. Though the nuns put it more delicately, the two were entwined like a pair of lovers. His arms were round her and one of the hind legs was thrown over his. I make no comment. Did he in the moment of death dream that he embraced his love? Or did he approach some transcendental reality when he wrote 'she had loved, therefore she is'?

Afterword

A Household Name

There was a time when Geoffrey Household really was a household name, or at least in households where good thriller writing was appreciated and other names such as John Buchan, Eric Ambler and Ian Fleming were bandied about.

I first came across the name on the cover of a paperback edition of *A Rough Shoot*, a thriller written before I was born but now appearing in orange Penguin livery (rather than the traditional green indicating crime and mystery) with a stylish modern art graphic cover by Charles Raymond. It must have been that cover which attracted me – I was 12 and spending all my pocket money on thrillers – because I knew nothing of the film of the book (made in 1953 starring Joel McCrea and Herbert Lom with a script written by Eric Ambler) and had never heard of the author.

After reading this short, sharp tale set mostly in darkest Dorset and populated by English country gentlemen carrying shotguns (as well as the odd foreign agent), I was, however, determined to find out more about this author which meant, in those pre-Google days, a trip to the local library. There, every reference I found pointed me firmly to an even older thriller; something called *Rogue Male*, which although first published in 1939 was not difficult to come by as it had remained in print more or less ever since – until recently the only Household title to do so, sadly.

With *Rogue Male* I was hooked, not only by the story but also by the story of the book's publication, which was almost as sensational.

Initially published in three instalments in the *Atlantic Monthly* magazine, *Rogue Male* tells of an assassination attempt, scandalously in peacetime, on a European dictator – clearly Adolf Hitler, though he is never named – by an aristocratic English gentleman and big game hunter. When published in book form in the UK, publication date just happened to be September 1st 1939, the day Hitler invaded Poland and *Rogue Male* was instantly on the way to becoming a classic and was quickly filmed by Fritz Lang in Hollywood under the title *Man Hunt*.

If *Rogue Male*, thanks to its subject matter and immaculate timing, is the book which made Geoffrey's name household, it did not profit the author in the short term for he had already been recruited by British Intelligence for special services overseas. He was not to return to England, and fiction writing, for six years. In his 1958 autobiography *Against The Wind*, Household tells the story in characteristic disarming fashion of how he received on 20th August 1939 a telegram from the War Office requesting him to report within 24 hours: 'The urgency surprised and flattered me. No one had ever demanded me within twenty-four hours; next week was always enough.'

The reason Geoffrey Household, by then a 38-year-old Territorial Army reservist, should be so in demand by a War Office still technically at peace was due to his rather unconventional life up to then and it was that life experience which was to shape and permeate his fiction.

After reading English Literature at Oxford, but graduating with no plans and no ambition, he drifted into a position as a trainee banker with the Franco-British Ottoman Bank in Bucharest, Romania – a job he accepted 'with joy and excitement, knowing nothing more of banks than that they were institutions upon which one drew a cheque hoping that it would be paid.'

During four years of youthful, carefree, hedonism, Household never once visited the oil fields of Romania or even learned more Romanian 'than was necessary to call a cab' and in 1926 relocated to Spain to try a fresh career as an importer of bananas. He then moved to the United States 'just in time for the Depression' and subsequently became a traveller in printer's inks in South America. During his wanderings he tried his hand at writing children's stories, finding some success in the U.S. and published his first novel in 1937 as he finally returned to live in England.

When, in that summer of 1939, the War Office summoned him for 'special duties' in MI(R) [Military Intelligence (Research), later to become part of the famous Special Operations Executive] it was, to his utter surprise, because of his experiences of Romania, fifteen years before, now that the Ploesti oilfields were clearly going to be of immense strategic value to an aggressive Nazi Germany.

It was probably a slightly bemused Captain Household who found himself shipped to Egypt, still in peacetime, to begin a clandestine life in the Balkans. As a fluent Spanish-speaker by now, he had half-expected that his 'special duties' would have consisted, romantically, of organising Basque or Catalan guerrillas to rise up against General Franco's Fascists. Instead, he found himself posing as an Insurance Agent and travelling via Palestine, the Lebanon and Turkey, to (neutral) Romania where his orders were to plan the destruction of the oilfields in the event of a German invasion – just as his novel *Rogue Male* was receiving great critical acclaim and success back home.

However, the plans of Household's amateur, but very willing, group of saboteurs were compromised in July 1940 when a French agent who was aware of them was arrested by the Gestapo in Paris. And as the Germans, Hungarians and Russians began to carve up Romania, Household and his Polish driver made a final defiant journey into occupied Transylvania in a British Legation car proudly flying the Union Jack.

Ordered back to Cairo in September 1940, Household volunteered for a posting in Field Security with the British army in Greece on the grounds that: 'I knew my way around Athens, could read a menu in Greek and choose from it intelligently.'

It is doubtful if he had much time to visit the restaurants of Athens, as the Germans invaded in April 1941 and Captain Household joined the British retreat and evacuation from Greece, hotly pursued by Nazi dive-bombers across terrain which would, forty years later, feature in *Rogue Justice*.

From that point, Household insisted he was a 'non-combatant' for the rest of the war, remaining in army Field Security and serving in Jerusalem and Beirut (whilst the film *Man Hunt* was playing in cinemas back in England) and Baghdad in Iraq, returning to Europe in 1945 for one final, traumatic posting to North Germany where he saw the liberation of Sandbostel concentration camp.

Demobbed from the army in July 1945, Household found himself having to more or less start again as a writer after six years abroad, or as he put it, back at the bottom of the snakes-and-ladders publishing game. From then, right up to his death in 1988, he produced thirty books – thrillers, picaresque novels, children's stories, science fiction and collections of short stories – all in a distinctive style which brought comparisons from the critics with the writing of Fielding, Defoe and Robert Louis Stevenson.

Yet it is for *Rogue Male* which he remains most famous and though publishers pressed him for a sequel for decades, it was not until, at the age of 80, that he began writing *Rogue Justice*. And just as the book, as well as being a cracking thriller of chase, flight and revenge, is a summation of the life and motivation of the once-anonymous Rogue Male – whom we now know to be Raymond Ingelram – it is also a summary of Household's personal beliefs forged by his cosmopolitan existence in the 1920s and 30s and his time as a soldier.

In *Rogue Justice* we learn that Ingelram is 'an agreeable dinner guest (with) no political opinions whatsoever' and that he is a man with no use for democracy, but who detests dictatorships. Both descriptions, I suspect, could easily have been applied to Household himself who often referred to himself as a 'romantic anarchist'. Certainly he had a loathing of state control on individual liberties, which he saw as inseparable from socialism, and admitted that 'In argument with politicians I am always beaten. I cannot express what I believe, whereas they express what they cannot possibly believe.' But his real hatred was reserved for Hitler and the Nazis and for what they had done to 'our once sweet Europe' and it is this passionate hatred which he gives his doomed hero Ingelram, with the added fuel of a very personal loss.

Even before the declaration of war in 1939, Geoffrey Household declared that 'My feeling for Nazi Germany had the savagery of a personal vendetta'. His autobiography records how he had 'watched the gropings of my Europe back towards the lights which had gone out in 1914'. Despite the economic depression, the lights of his Europe had flickered into life, only to be extinguished by aggressive Nazism.

Household's passionate 'Europeanism' is a constant theme in all his writing and the romantic nostalgia he felt for the old, noble, Europe of two empires (Hapsburg and Ottoman) is an integral theme of *Rogue Justice* and crucial to the psychology of his hero Raymond Ingelram, whose mother we learn was

Austrian, 'descended from the kings of Bohemia' with estates in Slovakia, The partisans Ingelram encounters on his bloody quest for justice represent 'the provinces of the vanished empire' and, when fighting alongside Poles, Czechs, Romanians and Austrians, he notes that 'we remained Europeans and men of honour. For me as for my ancestors, frontiers are only a nuisance.'

No one could ever have accused Geoffrey Household, on the surface the ultimate 'hunting, shooting, fishing English country squire' of being a 'Little Englander' for his liberal pan-Europeanism permeated his writing. His protagonists often have dual nationalities or mixed backgrounds, as in *Fellow Passenger* (1952), *Watcher in the Shadows* (1960) or *The Last Two Weeks of Georges Rivac* (1978), yet in the best of them is always a strong strain of stiff-upper-lipped English gentleman.

Nowhere more so than in Raymond Ingelram who personifies the English gentleman in *Rogue Male* and by the time we meet him in *Rogue Justice* has perfected the cool, very British (English) attitude of self-depreciation when under fire. Observing the use of the sub-machine gun (disparagingly referred to as 'a hosepipe'), Ingelram casually remarks 'The carefully aimed shot seemed to have become unfashionable in modern tactics' and later, when he tries 'a little north-west frontier stuff' at an enemy armoured column, he observes the retaliation casually: 'It was my first experience of a mortar – evidently a useful weapon for keeping a sniper on the move.'

For all Ingelram's self-imposed chivalrous rules of war – at one point he declares his private war over as he has crossed into Italian-occupied territory and he has no quarrel with Italians – we are left in no doubt that this is a vendetta which can only end in death, for Ingelram's sole aim is to avenge that 'dark, slender lioness of love and courage', his one true love tortured by the Gestapo ('she had never been allowed the chance to kill herself'), the event which had sparked his initial attempt to assassinate Hitler in *Rogue Male*.

The violence of the vendetta reaches the proportions of a pagan blood sacrifice and yet, when all seems lost and our hero contemplates suicide, the memory of his dead love – that 'dark and lovely lioness' – seems to appear to him and say, gently, 'Not yet, not yet'. Our hero's quest is, ultimately, nihilistic and doomed, just as it was from the start when the anonymous big-game hunter first placed Hitler in his telescopic sight.

Even though Ingelram does not expect (or want to) survive, his story is, quintessentially, a romantic one and, taken together, *Rogue Male* and *Rogue Justice* form an astonishing achievement: a multi-layered story disguised as an action thriller.

Despite the forty-year gap in writing, *Rogue Justice* is a superb coda to Household's classic *Rogue Male* and the two books together show his writing to be in a class well beyond that of the run-of-the mill thriller.

Mike Ripley,
July 2011.